Leo Kessler is a familiar name to readers of war fiction. In addition to his numerous superselling war series, he is the author of several non-fiction works and of the screenplay *Breakthrough*. A remarkably energetic writer, he lives in Germany between bouts of travelling. He is, of course, the only biographer personally authorised by Otto Stahl.

Also by Léo Kessler:
THE IRON FIST
THE TRAITORS
WOLF
BREAKTHROUGH

In the SS Assault Regiment Wotan series:
SS PANZER BATTALION
DEATH'S HEAD
CLAWS OF STEEL
GUNS AT CASSINO
THE DEVIL'S SHIELD
HAMMER OF THE GODS
FORCED MARCH
BLOOD AND ICE
THE SAND PANTHERS
COUNTER-ATTACK
PANZER HUNT
SLAUGHTER GROUND
HELLFIRE
FLASHPOINT
CAULDRON OF BLOOD

In the *Black Cossacks* series:
THE BLACK COSSACKS
SABRES OF THE REICH
MOUNTAIN OF SKULLS

In the *Stormtroop* series:
STORMTROOP
BLOOD MOUNTAIN
VALLEY OF THE ASSASSINS
RED ASSAULT
HIMMLER'S GOLD

In the *Rommel* series:
GHOST DIVISION
MASSACRE

Leo Kessler

Otto's Phoney War

Futura
Macdonald & Co
London & Sydney

A Futura Book

First published in Great Britain by
Macdonald Futura Publishers in 1981
Reprinted 1982

ISBN 0 7088 2027 1

Photoset by
Rowland Phototypesetting Ltd,
Bury St Edmunds, Suffolk
and printed in Great Britain by
Hazell Watson & Viney Ltd,
Aylesbury, Bucks

Futura Publications
A Division of
Macdonald & Co (Publishers) Ltd
Maxwell House
74 Worship Street
London EC2A 2EN

'My experience is that the gentlemen who are the best behaved and the most sleek are those who are doing the mischief. We cannot be too sure of anybody.'

Field Marshal Ironsides, 1940

'Gatsby believed in the green light, the orgiastic future that year by year recedes before us. It eluded us then, but no matter-tomorrow we will run faster, stretch out our arms farther . . . And one fine morning.'

Scott Fitzgerald, The Great Gatsby.

AUTHOR'S NOTE

I first heard of the remarkable Otto Stahl, the first section of whose racy memoirs appear in these pages, three years ago now. It was at the International Book Fair held annually in Frankfurt, West Germany, where British and American publishers, who see each other virtually every week in London and New York, pay expensive air fares and exorbitant hotel fees, in order to greet one another like long-lost friends in those booming Germanic display halls, heady with the smell of duty-free whisky – and money.

My London publisher, one of the Eton-Oxford sort, which will explain a lot to those who know the type, had long promised me an expensive lunch at the Fair. I should have been wiser. We ended up eating our over-cooked *bratwurst* and dry roll outside on a wooden bench next to the mobile snack-bar. 'Dining *al fresco*,' he called it charmingly. It was snowing lightly at the time. But then all rich publishers are like that, especially the Eton-Oxford sort. They always maintain it's the 'fault of the Accounts Department'. One thing, apart from a streaming head-cold, did come of the 'lunch' however. My publisher told me of his first encounter with Otto.

Apparently he had met the redoubtable Otto (he had

long forgotten his last name) when he had been a small boy in Vienna in the early fifties before the Four Power Control Commission had left Austria. Otto seemingly had been down on his luck at that time and was working for my publisher's father as a chauffeur (today, with what I know now, I suspect Otto was probably only using the job with an important British official as a cover for his extensive black market activities at that time). At all events Otto had intrigued the English boy with his tales of his wartime exploits, unheroic and infamous as they were. Now years later, my English publisher had forgotten most of them, save one.

In 1943 when Otto had been on the run from the SS he had 'taken a dive' and become the driver to the Inspector General, Infantry, of the German Army. The general had driven from Vienna (later I was to discover that Otto had had a predilection for 'taking a dive' in the Austrian capital) to Southern Russia to inspect his brave 'stubble-hoppers'. There Otto with his sharp nose for impending danger had soon seen that a tremendous debacle loomed ahead. Thus, one day when the general had commanded, 'Driver, take the car home,' meaning that Otto should drive it from the frontline back to the general's rear HQ, a couple of kilometres away, Stahl had interpreted the order literally. The General resided in Vienna; therefore that was home. He turned the big grey Horch around and drove straight back to Vienna, some twelve hundred kilometres to the rear, stopping only for fuel. That autumn the Inspector General and some half a million of his 'brave stubble-hoppers' went into the bag, but not Otto. He was safe in Vienna, enjoying the ample charms of the general's housemaid, and occasionally the Inspector General's youngish wife, who had no sense of class-distinction.

The episode intrigued me and during the years that followed I kept hearing similarly fascinating little stories both about 'Otto X's' wartime career and his post-war exploits. But still he remained a shadowy figure. My English publisher remembered him as very tall. But then all adults seem tall to small boys. A cockney informant recalls him as shrunken and bowed in his trench-coat and felt hat, pulled down well over his face, when they had first met outside King's Cross Station to begin their talks about financing a robbery. An ancient *SD* man remembered him as 'a typical SS officer, medium-sized and an arrogant swine, like they all were those days. Holy strawsack, he used to look at me through that monocle of his, as if I'd just crawled out of the woodwork!'

The thought of Otto wearing a monocle had shaken me a little, but still the SD man did add one little bit of description which tallied with that of the others. 'But you couldn't forget his eyes though . . . they were bright-blue and very intelligent. Just by looking at them, you could tell the arrogant swine had never lost a trick in his whole damned life!'

So it was that I wasn't altogether surprised when he spoke to me (apparently by accident in that remote Spanish coastal resort last winter); instinctively, I knew that the elderly German who seemed to know my name – and my profession – could only be the redoubtable Otto Stahl. Those sparkling, intelligent, winning blue eyes were a dead giveaway. Nor was I surprised too when he 'volunteered' to tell me his 'story', as he called it with that disarming crooked smile of his. Of course, there were 'certain conditions' to be met, and he reeled them off fluently like a salesman trying to sell you life-assurance. He had them all worked out, as if he had been thinking about the matter for a long, long time. His 'story' would be 'sensational' . . .'bawdy'. . . 'zany' . . .'all knickers and knobs'. . . . He sounded like a cheap publisher's publicity blurb.

At first I wasn't convinced. One could say intercourse had taken place, but without conception. Yet there was no denying Otto's crooked, slightly cynical charm; and the tales he told were really quite remarkable. He seemed to have been everywhere, done and seen everything. 'Otto once got the iron cross from Hitler for fucking a Dutch countess during the Battle for Holland,' he would announce in that oblique manner of his with a little grin. Or, 'Did you know that old Father Christmas, Admiral Canaris, head of the wartime German Secret Service to you, Leo, cooked and served me my dinner – in a chef's tall hat – the first time I ever met him?' he would say while I stared at him in open-mouthed disbelief.

Later when I was 'sold' and started to check his seemingly impossible tales, I found out that most of them were true. Hitler *had* awarded him the iron cross – and the knight's cross too! What Otto omitted to mention was that both of them were speedily taken away from him again when the authorities, to their consternation, found out exactly *how* he had won them. Admiral Canaris, the little spy-master with his two dachshunds and gay North African body-servant, *had* been wont to cook his subordinates' dinners, complete with chef's high cap and apron. And so on . . .

There in that remote winter resort within the confines of 'Rocki's Place' where Otto drank his breakfast-champagne – 'the strain of creation', he would plead as an excuse for the mid-morning tippling – it began to become clear to me that Otto had seen a side of the history of World War Two reserved normally to chambermaids, mistresses and discreet doctors of medicine, people not given usually to writing their memoirs. He had seen the great, with their knickers down, and recognised them for what they were. 'The bad jokes of Fortune: village pierrots yesterday, arbiters of life and death today, tomorrow's keepers of public latrines,' as Juvenal has it.

Otto began to grow upon me. He had been – and undoubtedly still was – a rogue, but a charming one. As he was wont to say himself to explain away his behaviour in that war of so long ago: 'In the Bible, Leo, it says that there was both a good thief and a bad thief on Calvary and the good thief went rapidly to heaven.' I doubt if Otto has ever read the Holy Script in all his life, but I don't doubt for one instant that when his time comes he will follow the Good Thief in the upwards direction . . .

Leo Kessler, Denia-las-Rotas, Spain.
Spring, 1980.

ONE : OTTO GOES OUT INTO THE WORLD

'Often most valuable clues can be picked up by spies who get beneath windows and peer in at the corners at critical times.'

William Le Queux

ONE

'*Morgen Leute!*' *Oberstabsarzt* Kieler croaked.

'*Morning Senior Staff Doctor!*' three hundred hoarse young voices bellowed back, their breath rising in a grey fog about their faces in the icy examination room.

Senior Staff Doctor Kieler hobbled forward a little, the sabre which he affected under his white medical smock slapping against his highly polished riding boots. Behind the ancient white-haired doctor, his juniors advanced apprehensively, as if they expected him to collapse at any moment. Kieler halted again and adjusted his pince-nez to stare hard with rheumy eyes at the young men, all of them stark naked, with their medical examination sheet held rigidly in front of their genitals as regulations prescribed.

'Today,' he commenced, using the same speech he had been giving since the beginning of the summer when it had become pretty clear that the Fuhrer intended to go to war over Poland, 'you are to be given the great honour of becoming a soldier. Not any old kind of a soldier, but a member of the Greater German Army.'

Someone in the back row of the naked young men farted.

Kieler's wrinkled face flushed angrily. 'If I catch the man who made that disgusting noise, I'll sew his arse up so that from then onwards he'll be shitting out of his ears!'

The terrible threat had its effect. Now the recruits listened to the senior staff doctor's set speech in complete silence, not even daring to shiver in that terrible cold.

'All of you are perfectly fit,' Kieler announced. 'There is absolutely no need to examine you for military service, but regulations demand that we must do so and so it will be done.' He raised the index finger of his grey-gloved hand in warning. 'However, there will be some among you, rogues and folk-parasites, who will maintain that they are unfit. They will state they are blind in one eye, are deaf, have weak hearts, rotten stomachs and all the rest of those idle excuses such low individuals always have prepared.' Kieler's voice rose. 'It will be of no use. Even malingerers of that kind will be given the honour of joining the *Wehrmacht* and laying down their miserable lives on the holy field of battle for our beloved Fuhrer, Adolf Hitler. I am, therefore, warning such carrion here and now that the eagle eye of *Oberstabsarzt* Kieler will be upon them. And nothing has ever escaped that terrible optic in fifty years of service to the Fatherland!'

Behind him one of the juniors sighed; the Old Man was as blind as a bat. The Medical Corps hadn't been able to trust him with a scalpel these twenty years or more.

'*Gut!*' Kieler barked and turned his back on the naked young men, 'Let the mustering commence!'

The juniors carried out their tasks with bored efficiency. Little rubber hammers testing reflexes. Quick search of pubic, armpit and head hair for lice. A swift touch of the stethoscope. A gloved finger in the anus for piles. A cough to check for rupture. A disdainful holding up of the penis at the end of a pencil. Stamp after rubber-stamp slammed down on the recruit's paper as he progressed in red-faced confusion from doctor to doctor, unwittingly passing from his comfortable, careful, civilian existence into that terrible field-grey machine that might one day soon ask him to put up his head and have it shot at. And all the while the ancient senior staff officer creaked rustily around the big hall, trailing his over-large sabre behind him on the floor, haughtily dismissing desperate hollow-chested consumptives, half-blind men who blundered from table to table with difficulty, half-wits from whose slack lips saliva ran down weak, unshaven chins; malingerers all, who would soon be all right when the Army began to build them up with plenty of good food, exercise and fresh air.'

It was just after a young blond man had fallen to the floor in what appeared to the juniors to be an epileptic fit, though *Oberstabsarzt* Kieler diagnosed the man's condition to be the 'result of over-excitement at the glorious prospect of being allowed to join the Greater German Army', that a polite voice at his elbow enquired, 'Stahl, Otto, respectfully requesting permission to speak to the Senior Staff Doctor on a private matter, sir!'

Kieler took his eyes off the naked man writhing back and forth on the floor, his body glazed with sweat, chunks of half-digested food vomiting from his gaping mouth, and creaked round slowly. A handsome young man stood there rigidly at attention, long Germanic face glowing with perfect health, body firm and muscular, obviously that of a trained athlete.

But it was the young man's eyes that caught Kieler's attention: they were bright-blue, gleaming with intelligence, and somehow winning, as if their owner had never suffered a single defeat in all his life. Kieler told himself that they were the eyes of a happy man.

'Yes, Stahl,' he said, his ancient face wrinkling into a smile of pleasure at what he saw. *Nomen es omen*, eh, steel in body and Steel in name.'

'I only wish it were so, sir,' the young naked man replied. 'It has always been my greatest dream to be able to serve our Fuhrer as an ordinary field-grey.' He sighed. 'Alas, sir, I don't think that will be possible. That is why I would like to speak with you privately, sir.'

Kieler's smile vanished. 'What do you mean, Stahl? You look to me in perfect condition, healthy as a young bull. I don't doubt one bit that you've been able to find enough young women to service with that monstrous thing hanging between your legs.'

'Oh, that's all right, sir,' Stahl replied, a sad look on his handsome face now. 'In my time I am sure I have helped to produce some of those children Germany will need in the future. It's not that at all. It's my arm, you see.'

'Your arm – what's wrong with it?' He indicated Stahl's left arm with his sabre. 'Raise it!'

Obediently Stahl did so, the muscles rippling the length of the brawny limb, to reveal a tuft of thick black hair under the armpit.

Kieler adjusted his pince-nez and stared at the arm short-sightedly. 'All right,' he announced finally. 'Nothing there.'

'Yes, sir, I know. But it's not that arm which is giving me trouble, sir. It's the right arm – my firing arm.'

'What's wrong with it?'

'It's the green and blue swelling underneath it,' Stahl said softly and any observer more acute than the senile senior staff doctor would have noticed that at that particular moment an element of tension had crept into Stahl's voice and those winning eyes of his had suddenly grown wary and a little anxious.

'Green and blue swelling?' Kieler echoed puzzled. 'That's rather strange in that particular spot. Let me have a look at it, Stahl. Don't worry, my boy,' he forced a smile. 'Whatever it is, we'll soon have the problem solved. Never fear, my boy.'

Slowly, gingerly almost, as if he were experiencing great pain doing so, Otto Stahl raised his arm, his eyes fixed almost hypnotically on Kieler's face, until finally the arm was stretched straight in the air and the doctor could see the large object taped by red sticking-plaster to the inside of the biceps.

'Why,' he stuttered, peering through his glasses at the object. 'It seems to be . . . a bundle of notes, Stahl!'

Stahl flashed a quick look to left and right. None of the other doctors were looking in their direction. 'To be exact, sir, it's two thousand reichsmark in hundred mark bills.'

'But I don't . . . understand, Stahl.'

'Easy, sir.' Now the eyes were warm and winning once more. 'Due to certain other pressing engagements elsewhere, sir, I would like to be excused from military service.'

'Excused?' Kieler stuttered. 'But you're perfectly fit. How can one excuse you?'

'It's the swelling under my arm, sir . . . It could be yours – to lance if you could see your way to arrange this matter for me.'

'A bribe! Are you trying to bribe me, Stahl?' Kieler exploded.

'Easy, sir,' Stahl said soothingly. 'We shouldn't put it as crudely as that, sir. I mean I know you have certain extra expenditures for that little house in Berlin-Wedding, and I thought, perhaps those two thousand marks might help out with Fraulein Krause's . . . domestic expenses.'

'*Fraulein Krause*,' the ancient military doctor breathed incredulously. '*You* know Fraulein Krause?'

'And how!' Stahl said to himself, but aloud he said as polite and discreet as ever 'Yessir, I did have occasion to meet your – er – little friend . . .'

It had been as easy as falling off a log.

As soon as he had received the dread summons to attend for his medical, he had made his decision to find some way out. As he had told his mother, known locally in Berlin-Kreuzberg as the 'Witch', on account of her beard, cat and the big wart that balanced precariously on the end of her hooked nose, 'Mama, old Hitler isn't going to get me as cheap cannon-fodder.' To which she had replied with a shrill cackle, revealing the long solitary yellow tooth that graced her gums, 'I'll lend you my broom and you can just fly away my son!'

But Otto Stahl had had no intention of taking a dive. Sooner or later, he knew, the authorities would find him and he had no wish to spend the rest of his days in the dreaded military prison at Torgau. Instead he had soon found out who led the medical committee responsible for the mustering in his district. A little discreet shadowing of the ancient doctor with his preposterous dragging sabre and over-large riding boots had led him straight to Fraulein Krause's modest little house in the working-class suburb of Berlin-Wedding, and he had not needed the Witch's crystal-ball to know what *Oberstabsarzt* Kieler was doing, with the ample-breasted gushing typist in her mid-thirties. As he remarked to his mother, 'You can't tell me, Mama, he's holding her hand and taking her temperature down there.'

'It ain't her hand he's holding, of course not, Otto.' The Witch had made an explicit gesture with her dirty middle finger and cackled so that he had been forced to shake his head in mock wonder and say, 'I don't know you old bag, ever since you've stopped pounding the pavement, I declare you've got worse. Your sexual imagination is running away with you.' The Witch had blown him a toothless kiss. One day later he had knocked at Fraulein Krause's door, a bunch of cheap red roses in his hand, dressed in his best suit, stuttering apologies that he had obviously knocked at the wrong one, spinning the old tale that the beautiful woman he had met the night before at Tempelhof – 'Of course, Fraulein, not as beautiful as you by far,' – had given him this address.

It was clear now, naturally, that she had stood him up. 'So' – he had given the confused typist the roses and that winning, if sad smile of his –'why don't you accept them, *gradiges Fraulein*? I have no use for them – now.' And he had turned to go.

It had worked like a charm; it always did.

'But I couldn't accept such beautiful flowers just like that,' she had protested. 'Couldn't I offer you a little drink at least?'

'Well, just one,' he had replied and followed her inside.

Five minutes later they were wrestling on the couch together under the forbidding look of the Fuhrer who hung on the wall, posing as a medieval knight, complete with flag and horse. Another five and he had her bra off and was toying with her massive breasts while she lolled there, head thrown back, eyes closed, mouth opened like that of a stranded, dying cod. Her knickers followed too in due course, carelessly flung over the Fuhrer's portrait. Within thirty minutes of having entered her apartment, Fraulein Krause was writhing on the carpet, gasping she would surely die if he took "it" out now.

Two hours later he had departed, swearing undying love, taking with him all the information he needed to know about the head of the medical committee, including a rather peculiar story of one of the ancient doctor's nastier habits in bed, plus Fraulein Krause's pearls, which had fetched a cool two thousand reichsmarks at a fence he knew in Kreutzberg.

As he had said to his mother, 'I've got him! The shitting bonemender better let me go, or it'll be the worse for him.'

'Yes, Otto,' she had replied, looking at him as if she were seeing him for the first time. 'You're a smart lad. You'll go far. You see you inherited my brain, not yer father's.'

'What father?' had been Otto Stahl's reply . . .

'Well, *Herr Oberstabsarzt*?' Otto demanded.

'What if I don't do as you wish?' the doctor quavered,

with an attempt at defiance.

Smiling winningly, Stahl bent forward and whispered something in the other man's hairy ear.

The doctor's bottom lip dropped stupidly and for a moment Otto thought he might cry. 'But you wouldn't tell anybody *that*?' he exclaimed. 'I'm an old man . . . I have to do such things . . . to get it . . . Well, you understand?'

'Of course, *Herr Oberstabsarzt*. We all have our little peculiarities. But you must admit it is a little strange, not to say fancy, eh?'

'All right, damn yer impudent eyes,' Kieler snarled and reaching up, ripped off the plaster from Otto's arm, hastily concealing the bundle of notes, 'I'll certify you unfit for military service, you cunning devil. But I'm warning you, Stahl, you'd better get as far away from Berlin as possible. One day you'll be re-mustered and you might find that the head of the medical commission is not as humane and understanding as good old Kieler.'

'Thank you for the advice, dear Doctor,' a happy Otto said, holding up his sheet for the *Oberstabsarzt*'s signature. 'Stahl, Otto, will be seen in the capital of the Greater German Reich no more. Forthwith I shall leave my native stamping grounds to seek my fortune in the wide, wide world.'

Kieler sniffed but said nothing, his mind suddenly filled with his problem. Perhaps a *kneip* water-cure might help him; the old cures were often the best ones.

Naked as he was, Otto clicked to attention and raised the paper to his forehead in mock salute. 'Good-bye, Little Doctor, and do try to improve your performance with Fraulein Krause. She is so grateful for even the *smallest* of pleasures, if you follow me?'

And with that he was gone, leaving a glowering *Oberstabsarzt* Kieler staring at his broad back, as if he might be tempted to draw his sabre and run him through at any moment, sauntering through the big room without a care in the world, waving a fond farewell to the downtrodden young men who were now officially members of the *Grossdeutsche Wehrmacht*. 'Have a good war, fellers,' he said and disappeared into the changing-rooms.

Otto had commenced his adventures.

TWO

Engineer Sergeant Georg Forz, nicknamed 'The Fart-Cannon', was pleased with himself as he stood there on the hillock, watching the new day start in the Eifel hills.

It had been a good night. Walburga, his plump wife, had been drunkenly affectionate after the NCOs' party. For once she had not refused him on account of her 'migraine', as she always called it. Afterwards he had fallen into a deep sleep in which he had dreamed his favourite dream: the surprise visit of the Fuhrer to his section of the new fortified line. During it, the Fuhrer had been so impressed by his work that he had spontaneously awarded him the Service Cross, Third Class.

Now as the red ball of the sun hung over the wooded hills, he could already hear the bold marching song of his favourite bunch of workers, the young men of the *Arbeitsdienst** setting off for a new day of work on the secret fortifications that were now beginning to stretch over valley and hill from Aachen on the Dutch frontier to Schaffenhausen on the Swiss. And then there they were, stamping by in perfect formation, hard muscular bodies naked to the waist, their polished spades carried over their shoulders like rifles, gleaming in the first rays of the sun, column after column of them, hoarse young voices bellowing out their proud patriot song:

* In Nazi Germany, all men and women between the ages of seventeen and eighteen had to spend six months in public service, mostly in labour camps.

'Unsere Fahne flattert uns voran
In die Zukunft ziehn wir Mann fur Mann
Wir marschieren fur Hitler durch Nacht und durch Not
*Mit der Fahne der Jugend fur Freiheit und Brot.'**

'Great God,' an admiring Forz whispered to himself, as he watched the handsome, half-naked young men disappear into the forests, 'if I weren't straight as a die, I could take the vaseline to some of them. They're beautiful!'

'Sergeant Forz,' a weak hesitant voice broke into the bull-like NCO's sexual reveries, 'have you a minute, Sergeant?'

Forz turned round. It was Wurm, his hunchbacked, bespectacled civvy clerk, who did most of the work in the engineering office, while Forz spent the day drinking beer and schnaps with his NCO cronies at the building sites and camps scattered all over the remote Eifel border-country.

For a long moment he looked down his big nose at the hunchback, blood-shot eyes full of contempt for what he saw there. 'Well, Wurm, what yer pissing yer pants about now, eh?'

Wurm rubbed his skinny yellow hands together, as if they were dirty. It was a common gesture of his when he was nervous – and he was always nervous in the early morning: at such a time Engineer Sergeant Forz was highly unpredictable, especially when Frau Forz had had one of her unfortunate 'migraines' again. Sometimes he was tempted to buy Forz a regular supply of aspirins to give her; it would make his life easier. 'It's the new civvy workers, sir,' he quavered. 'They've just reported for duty and I thought—'

'You know what thought did, Wurm?' Forz said heartily in high good humour. 'He thought he'd shat himself – *and he had*!' Forz bellowed with laughter at his

* 'Our flag flutters to our front. We're moving into the future, each man of us. We'll march for Hitler through night and trouble. With the flag of youth, for freedom and bread.

own humour and walloped Wurm such a blow on his hump that he almost fell into the foundations of one of the new bunkers that were springing up everywhere in these remote hills this summer. 'All right, Wurm, lead on. Let's have a look at the idle shits.'

The civilians, recruited from all parts of Germany for the massive building project, lounged against the wooden walls of the engineers' shack, enjoying the warming rays of the early sun, chatting quietly to one another, savouring the first cigarette of the new day.

Forz's big red face darkened even more. He halted abruptly so that Wurm ran into his broad back and planted himself, legs astride, big barrel-chest thrown out, and glowered at the motley crew of middle-aged civilians and pimply youths who made up his new gang.

'What do you think this is – a *Yiddish knocking shop or something*!' he bellowed suddenly, making one of the pimply youths swallow his cigarette with fright. 'Snap those brittle bones together, suck in those arse-cheeks, haul in those beer tumours, raise them turnips – and dowse those lung torpedoes! *At the double now!*'

Startled by the stream of commands pouring out of the infuriated giant's mouth, the motley crew of civilians shuffled into the position of attention; all save one – a bold-faced, young man with clear, winning eyes, who continued to lounge against the wall, quietly puffing away at his *Juno-Eckstein*, as if he had not heard one word.

Forz swallowed his spit and then strode forward slowly, taking his time, allowing the purple vein at his temple to tick, as if he might explode with anger at any moment, putting on the same act that had scared the pants off two generations of green recruits and earned him a fearsome reputation among the young soldiers who had had the misfortune to fall into his big beefy paws.

He paused, only half a metre away from the young man smoking, and puffed up his barrel-chest to its most impressive dimensions. 'Perhaps the gentleman is a little hard of hearing?' he said with deceptive softness, his piglike eyes glittering, using the old-fashioned, third-person form of address reserved for the upper classes.

'Not at all,' the young man answered easily in a thick fast manner which Forz identified as that of Berlin. 'In fact, I've got perfect hearing.' He dropped his cigarette and made a business of stubbing it out with his elegant, highly polished shoe. 'I heard every word you said, Sergeant.'

Behind Forz's broad back, the clerk's skinny hand flew to his mouth in alarm. Didn't the Berliner realise to whom he was talking? In one second, Forz would explode and then the shit would begin to fly.

'I see,' Forz said quietly. 'You heard everything I said?'

'That is correct, Sergeant.' The Berliner yawned, as if the whole business were beginning to bore him.

'You heard me order you fellows to assume the position of attention?'

The Berliner nodded and looked down at his nails.

'THEN WHY DIDN'T YOU?' Forz exploded, his face suddenly crimson with rage.

The Berliner was unmoved by the outburst. Instead he calmly wiped Forz's spittle from his handsome face and said quietly. 'Because Sergeant, we are civilians and we are not subjected to military discipline. Standing to attention is meant for toy soldiers, and not for civilians like us.'

Someone giggled and Wurm blanched, arm half-raised, as if he anticipated being struck forcibly at any moment. The Berliner must be completely mad!

'What did . . . did you say then?' Forz stuttered.

'Perhaps it's you who should see a doctor about his ears, Sergeant?' the Berliner suggested easily. 'I thought I spoke clearly enough?'

'You . . . you . . . Forz quivered with impotent rage, unable to vent his anger on this insolent swine who had had the audacity to insult him like this . . . By the Great

God and all His Triangles, I'm going to learn you! I'll have you up to your hooter in shit every damn minute of the day! You're gonna wish you had never encountered Engineer-Sergeant Forz.' He ripped the note book from the cuff of his tunic and flapped it open with an enfuriated gesture. 'Now then what's your name! . . . Come on, out with it, man. Snap to!'

'Stahl . . . Stahl, Otto,' the Berliner answered, his face revealing no fear at the big NCO's angry outburst. 'You can call me, Otto, if you like, seeing we're getting off to such a friendly start.'

Forz gasped and he almost dropped his pencil with rage. '*Gott im Himmel!*' he cursed in a strangled voice, big head twisted to one side, as if he were having the greatest of difficulty in breathing. 'That's enough . . . As soon as I dismiss you, you're gonna get a shovel from the shed and you're gonna clean out every damn shit-house from here to Aachen, if it takes you the rest of your life. *You're gonna eat shit, drink shit, live shit and dream shit!* . . .' He swallowed hard, telling himself that if he didn't control himself in a moment, he'd have a heart attack.

The Berliner remained unmoved. 'Although I'd very much like to help you out with the thunder-boxes, Sergeant, it can't be done.'

'Can't be done?' a purple-faced Forz breathed.

'Yes, can't be done,' the other man answered calmly, reaching in his jacket and bringing out a piece of paper. 'This is the result of my Army-medical signed by *Oberstabsarzt* Kieler of Berlin's Third Military District. He attests that I am Grade-C Medical Category. You can read it here, if you wish, Sergeant.'

Blindly Forz stared at the paper, totally unable to comprehend it or to speak.

'So that means, Sergeant, I am only fit for light duties.' Otto smiled winningly at the dumbstruck NCO. 'I thought I might work in the office or perhaps, seeing an outdoor life might do my state of health some good, I could drive the company truck bringing up supplies from Aachen or the like. Yes,' he said happily, apparently warming to the idea. 'That would be nice. A fellow can see a lot of the countryside that way, can't he?'

Big paw clutching his side, Forz staggered to the office, unable to speak, indicating with his other hand that Wurm should take them over.

Otto watched him go and said mildly, 'Did I say something to offend him, fellows?'

Now it was midday. Behind the shed, the civilians, faces glazed with sweat from a morning's digging, spooned their thick pea soup up out of their metal messtins, washing it down with cold tea out of bottles, saying little; then they were too tired to talk.

Otto was as clean and as immaculate as he had been at dawn, for Sergeant Forz had been too angry to attempt to set him to work and Otto had spent most of the morning hanging around the company office, chatting with the little clerk Wurm whenever Sergeant Forz was not in sight.

Now the two of them stood on the hillock behind the shed, while Wurm pointed out the area to his companion. 'That's Holland over there – the Maastricht appendix, the officers call it, because that part of the cheeseheads' country is hanging into the Reich. And there, where the hills begin, that's Belgium.'

Otto searched the area for a few moments before announcing, 'But they don't seem to have any fortifications on their side of the frontier, Wurm.'

'They haven't, save for a few wooden bunkers and a couple of trench lines,' Wurm agreed.

'Then what's all this in aid of?' He indicated the great metal gun turret coming slowly out of the earth, followed an instant later by the cannon sliding its length from the cupola. 'What do we need that mole with an erection for, eh?'

Wurm gave the 'German look', a glance to left and right to find out whether anyone was listening to him.

Satisfied that they were not being overheard, he whispered nervously, 'I think we're gonna use this new *Westwall** to have a crack at the Polacks, while the soldiers hold off the Tommies and the French up here.'

'I 'spect you're right, Wurm,' the other man said, his handsome face suddenly gloomy. 'Berlin was full of rumours of war when I left.'

'What did you do in Berlin, Stahl?' Wurm asked deciding it was wiser to change the subject.

'Not much. What could a bloke like me do when his Old Lady is walking the pavement, or used to before she lost her biters, whose Old Man stayed one night and never returned, which makes me a bastard.' He smiled at the other man with disarming frankness, as if he confessed every day to a virtual stranger that he was a bastard. 'Besides I'm not in the Party and that's as bad as having leprosy as far as most employers go. So,' he shrugged expressively, 'what do you do? A little job here, a little job there.' He made a twisting gesture with his right hand, as if he were swiftly concealing some object behind his back. Wurm stared up at the other man in amazement. 'You mean – *you organised things*?' he gasped.

'Found them before they were lost, I prefer to say,' Otto agreed with a grin. 'Why not? Don't you know we're governed by a bunch of crooks? The only difference between them and me is that they've made being criminal legitimate.'

'You shouldn't say things like that, Stahl,' Wurm whispered urgently, dark eyes behind the thick-rimmed glasses, flickering anxiously left and right, as if there might well be a Gestapo-man just behind him. 'You can get into trouble, serious trouble.'

Otto gave him one of those winning smiles of his. 'Not Otto. He's just a little bit smarter than those crooks at the top, just one jump ahead.'

'I'm not altogether happy with our leadership my-

* German name for the Siegfried Line.

self,' Wurm said carefully. 'You see I'm a catholic. We all are around here. And in recent years the Party has treated our priests pretty rotten, forbidding them to preach from the pulpit, threatening them, and worse – the *camps*,' he whispered the word apprehensively, and bit his bottom lip, as if he had just suddenly realised he had said too much.

Otto laughed at the other man's obvious fear. 'You know I was a passionate Nazi myself up to four or five years ago when I was a kid. You see, as my Old Lady was on the pavement in Berlin, I was brought up by my grandfather in Stralsund on the Baltic. He was the old school, the Kaiser, Sedan Day and the Prussian Guard – he'd been in the Grenadiers. So it was understandable that I grew up just dying to become cannon-fodder for the Fuhrer when I was old enough. I dreamed of dying in a trapped U-boat under the North Sea, hurtling down in one last desperate dive in a Stuka, going over the top to slaughter frogs. Hell, I saw *Hitler Youth Quex** ten times over and cried each time when the communist stabbed him right at the end and he's lying there dying on the cobbles with the blood all over his face and he starts to sing the Hitler Youth Song. I used to bawl my eyes out!' Otto laughed softly at the memory. 'But then I grew up and grew up fast when it happened and I knew that they were pigs and killers and worse criminals than you'd find in any prison.' His face hardened. 'Then I knew I was going to have no more truck with their rotten system. I did a bunk from Grandfather, found the Old Lady in Berlin and that was that. I was in the organising business, for better or worse.'

'But what happened, Stahl?' Wurm asked. 'What made you change your mind about the Nazis?'

But before Otto could answer that question, Forz was shrilling his NCO's whistle to indicate the dinner-break was over and he was crooking his big finger at him with a malicious grin on his beer-flushed face that indicated

* A well-known Nazi propaganda film.

that he had finally found some way of taking his revenge on the damned Berliner who had insulted him so audaciously that dawn.

THREE

'But I don't want a servant,' Walburga whined, as she lay on the couch in her nightdress revealing her ample thighs and a goodly portion of her massive bosom, a bandage soaked in vinegar wrapped around her head. 'What should I do with a servant, especially a man? Men are always underfoot in a house. Besides,' she opened her eyes and flashed Forz a warning look, as he gazed at her thick white thighs with frank lust, 'he might attack me – you know, that way?' She pulled her gown down over her thighs. 'All men are pigs. They're always after that one thing.'

'He'd better not,' Forz said hotly, realising that Walburga was working up to one of her 'migraines' again; he'd be sleeping in the spare-room this night. 'I'd have the eggs off'n him with a blunt knife if he even laid his little finger on you, Walburga. No, don't you worry, my little *schnuggi*. You just give him the orders and he'll carry them out. Empty the pisspot in the morning, beat the carpets, carrying up the briquettes from the cellar, peel the potatoes for dinner – that sort of thing. Keep the cheeky bastard busy all the time while you have a good rest so that at night you can be fit and, well, you know what I mean?' he ended lamely, his big broad face suddenly red, as if with embarrassment.

'Yes, I know what you mean, you big horned-ox!' she said. 'That's all you ever think about.' She sniffed. 'For you, I'm just a thing to be used when your animal desires get too much for you.'

'My little cheetah, don't say things like that,' Forz answered hastily. 'You know I've only got your welfare at heart. Please, let me bring him in and see what you think. If you don't like him, I'll send him packing . . . There, have one of these chocolates I've just brought you.' Hastily he pushed the expensive box of chocolates in front of her.

'You can't bribe me, you know,' she said, picking up one of them and biting into it a little greedily. 'All right, wheel the fellow in.'

Forz didn't wait for her to change her mind. Swiftly he slipped outside into the corridor where Stahl was waiting, staring intently at a picture of Walburga in a woollen bathing suit which revealed her ample charms all too clearly.

'Get yer filthy optics off that photo!' he barked. 'I won't have you looking at the little woman in that manner.'

'In what manner?' Otto asked innocently.

'You know what I mean,' the big NCO snorted. 'As if yer were whipping her knickers off her and all . . . Now remember you are in the home of a senior NCO of the Greater German Army. We're good solid folk here, none of your Berlin trash. And I tell you this – for free, Stahl,' he said in sudden triumph. 'This is not going to be any cushy number, not with my wife. In this house we make fried taties out of shit – and don't you forget it. Now move those brittle bones!'

'I won't, Sergeant Forz,' Otto said easily and moved his 'brittle bones'.

'This is him, Walburga,' Forz said as the two of them stood poised at the door.

For what seemed a long time Walburga Forz did not seem to hear, busy as she was with the chocolates, biting into the ones she didn't particularly like and leaving them half-eaten, in favour of those she did like. But finally she deigned to look up.

Standing slightly to the rear of the big NCO, Otto winked at her and pursed his lips, as if he were about to plant a large kiss on her left breast which had almost slipped out of the loose gown.

She frowned, but she did not pull up her gown which she would have done if she had caught Forz staring at her body in that way. Instead she took up another chocolate, little finger spread out, and made a great play of eating it in what she considered a ladylike manner.

'What do you think, Walburga?' Forz asked anxiously.

'Ask him if he can iron clothes,' she said in a little demure voice. 'You know how the heat from ironing affects my migraine.'

'Of course . . . of course, my little sweetie,' Forz said hastily. 'All right, you heard Frau Forz,' he rapped to Otto. 'Can you iron?'

'Naturally, Sergeant,' Otto replied easily, his cheeky gaze running up and down the wife's body with what appeared to be undisguised admiration. 'I'm specially good with ladies' lingerie. I was taught to do ladies' pretty, intimate things by my old mother, who ran a little service for well-born ladies in Berlin,' Otto lied glibly, remembering the place the Witch had managed for lesbians behind the Anhalter Station when she had been unable to work the pavements herself. 'You can rely on me, Frau Forz.'

'Did you hear that, Walburga?' Forz said eagerly. 'He's very good with ladies' lingerie.'

'All right,' she said, appearing to be indifferent. 'I'll take him – on a week's trial, that is. If he's no good then, he's to go. *Klar?*'

'*Klar!*' Sergeant Forz agreed quickly and turned to Otto with an unholy grin on his broad face. 'Now you've had it, my lad,' he chortled, escorting him outside and closing the door on the woman reclining on the couch, cheeks bulging with chocolate, uneasy strange thoughts already beginning to flood through her mind. 'By God, Stahl, my Walburga will lead you a merry little dance, I'll be bound!'

Stahl nodded his head slowly, keeping his eyes

lowered so that the grinning NCO could not see the look in them. 'I expect yer right, Sergeant Forz,' was all he said.

Thus Otto became Frau Walburga Forz's house-servant, apparently kept busy all the day with the chores that the big blonde pressed upon him, for within the week he had lost a considerable amount of weight and at night, he headed straight for his bunk to collapse there in an exhausted sleep, as if he were completely worn out. Even on their first free Sunday, his comrades could not drag him out of bed to take the bus to Aachen and see the sights, in particular the whores who frequented the dingy cobbled streets behind the border city's *Hauptbahnhof*. 'Don't talk to me about women,' he moaned and held up his hands, as if to ward off some monstrous female or other. 'I've had enough this week. I've got them right up to here.' He drew an angry line underneath his nose. 'A real noseful!'

The sight of the skinny young civilian, dark circles of exhaustion under his eyes, beating the carpets wearily, staggering as he did so, gave Forz a great deal of satisfaction. More than once as he came home for his dinner, he would smirk and remark, 'I see she's keeping you at it, Stahl, eh?'

'That she is, Sergeant,' Otto would croak. 'That she *certainly* is!'

And the big NCO would go inside with a big grin on his drinker's face, telling himself that she was giving the new servant a really hard time; he was getting his own back on the cocky young Berliner one hundred per cent. There was only one fly in the ointment. As soon as they went to bed each night, Walburga would turn her back on him and fall immediately into a deep sleep, in spite of the fact that she had a servant to do the housework now and could spend her days lying on the couch, eating chocolates and reading the fifty-pfennig novelettes she favoured, which were always about mysterious handsome young aristocrats and simple, if beautiful, village maidens in love. It was all very puzzling and a bit frustrating. The only improvement he could note was that she no longer complained of her 'migraine', but then even that didn't mean very much, as she was always in a drugged sleep when he attempted to approach her. As he complained to his cronies of the sergeants' mess more than once, his big broad face puzzled and sad, 'There's no way of pleasing gash, comrades. Give 'em a little finger and they take the whole shitting hand.'

It was a sentiment with which an exhausted Otto could have only agreed.

Thus while a sorely plagued Otto apparently suffered the endless demands of Frau Walburga Forz in that remote corner of Germany, Berlin prepared for war. The comings and goings between the capitals of Western Europe were manifold. Diplomatic gentlemen in black jackets and striped pants hurried back and forth in an attempt 'to save the peace', as they invariably called their efforts, reading each other long 'communications', full of high-faluting, pompous phrases, knowing all the while that they were participants in a game, an absurd diplomatic game, being played for the benefit of the citizens of the nations which they represented.

For the European War had already been decided upon. In Warsaw, the apparent victim, Colonel Beck had resolved, almost eagerly, to commit national suicide: he would fight. In Paris, Daladier, the swarthy-faced grocer, had made the same decision, although he knew that half the French Army would collapse as soon as they heard the first shot fired in anger. In Moscow the Georgian dictator with the pock-marked face was already counting his chickens before they were hatched; he'd go to war, too, but through the back door. Let the Western powers fight each other to the bitter end; Poland would be his. Most amazingly of all the arch-appeaser

Chamberlain, he of the black Homburg and rolled umbrella, had made a 180 degree about-face, and was rattling sabres with the best of them. He was going to fight too.

They were all so eager to plunge Europe into another great war that Hitler, the dictator who had kept the Continent in fear for half a decade now, was suddenly confused and not a little fearful. Abruptly he began to lose his nerve. He postponed the attack on Poland once – and then again. 'What's their game, Ribbentrop?' he asked his Foreign Minister time and time again. '*What's their damn game?* . . .'

In that remote border country, strange games were now being played daily in Frau Forz's bedroom, behind those tightly drawn flowered curtains, and Otto's strength was being sapped hourly by the insatiable demands of Walburga Forz, she of the 'migraine', who had discovered late in life in the arms of the stranger from Berlin that the bed games she had once found so disgusting were really almost unbearably enjoyable. But it was the 'doctor game' which was the last straw for a sorely tried Otto and which decided him that his days as a house-servant were numbered.

On the bright sunny morning of Thursday 30 August 1939, Walburga Forz, completely naked and slightly tipsy (for she had taken to drinking cognac after breakfast now as soon as her husband had departed for work), welcomed a slightly apprehensive, tired Otto with open arms and the announcement, 'Today we play doctor, Otto!'

'Doctor?' he echoed.

'Yes, like the kids play down behind the woodshed when they think their parents are not looking,' she giggled and swayed a little unsteadily. She picked up the frilly white apron that lay ready on the bed and slipped into high-heeled shoes, while she bound the apron around her plump waist. 'You see, I'm the doctor . . .'

Gently she forced him back on the big bed, dominated by the portrait of Sergeant Forz on the wall, dressed in his best uniform, complete with ceremonial dagger and suitably martial look on his face, and slipped her wet tongue into his ear, 'and you're the patient.'

'Hey now wait a minute!' he protested, but already she was hurrying into the kitchen, laughing gaily as she went and muttering something about fetching her 'medical kit'.

A moment later she returned, smiling archly, her heaving breasts billowing like melons under the white apron, a bottle in one hand, complete with two glasses, and bandages, plus sticking-tape and scissors in the other.

'Hey, now what in three devils' names do you think—' She smothered his protest with a damp, open-mouthed kiss, pouring two glasses of *kognak* as she did so. 'There,' she breathed, her eyes gleaming and her face flushed, presenting him with a glass. 'Toss that down behind your collar in one go. *Ex!*' she commanded. 'Do as the doctor tells you, you naughty boy. You see that is your anaesthetic. We don't want our little patient to feel any pain, do we. Come on now. *EX!*'

'Oh sit on yer thumb!' Otto groaned, suddenly panicked by the sight of such obvious sexual eagerness; she was at it again. In one draught he drank the cognac. An instant later she started to claw open his flies with eager fingers.

Resigned to his fate, he let it happen. She started to draw down his trousers, over his waist, down his thighs along his stockinged feet, muttering all the while with tipsy pleasure, 'Don't wriggle, you naughty boy. The Doctor knows what's best for you. Behave yourself or I'll have to spank your bot—' Suddenly she gasped at the sight revealed to her greedy eyes. 'Oh dear!' she breathed in awe, taking a quick drink from her own glass, '*that* does look a nasty wound, a very nasty one indeed.' She took the pencil she had in her apron and cautiously touched it with the pencil. 'You poor boy,' she breathed, a mad look on her sweating purple face now. 'How you must be suffering! Don't worry though, the good Doctor will soon have you cured.'

'What you going to do, Walburga?' Otto cried, as she turned and fumbled with the bandages.

But she was no longer listening. Now she had gone completely into some private world, oblivious to him, concerned solely with her own bizarre, sexual fantasies.

What happened next would cause Otto occasional nightmares for years to come, even after he had killed men with his own bare hands and fled two thousand kilometres through war-torn Russia, with every man's hand against him.

Muttering crazily to herself, the sweat dripping from her puffed-up sweat-glazed face, her hair hanging down in wild disorder, she began to bandage him up, crooning now again something about 'this hurts me more than you, you naughty boy. So don't cry or the Doctor will be angry with you.'

In the end, Otto closed his eyes and gave up, letting her satisfy her desires in her own manner, trying not to hear the puffing and little groaning sounds she was now making, tormented as she was by some private ecstasy.

Finally she gave a kind of horselike whinny and he opened his eyes in alarm to see her sagging against the side of the bed, her nipples standing out like red bottle-tops, as if she might faint at any moment, her eye-lashes fluttering wildly, the sweat pouring down her face in streams.

'What—' Otto stopped short. Something like a large cocoon lay crosswise across his stomach, somehow sinister and not a little frightening. 'Look . . . look, what you've done to me!' he exclaimed in horror. 'My salami looks as if it's been through a meat-grinder.'

She shook her head several times, as if she were trying to wake up out of a deep trance, her eyes unable to focus, her tongue hanging out of the corner of her mouth like that of a cretin.

'Well?' he demanded. 'What are you going to do about

it, woman?' Angrily he sat up on the bed. 'For Chrissake, don't just stand there – do something!'

'The scissors,' she croaked, reaching for the instruments, with a hand that trembled badly.

'Are you crazy!' Otto cried wriggling to the other side of the bed to get out of her reach. 'With the kind of shakes you've got, you silly cow, you'd cut it right off!'

It was just then that the nightmare reached its crescendo. There was that well-known stamp of heavy Army boots coming down the gravel path that led to the little house.

Walburga's hand flew to her mouth in alarm.

'Holy Stawsack!' Otto cried. '*It's your old man – the Fart-Cannon!*' Frantically he grabbed his trousers and rolled from the rumpled bed, while Walburga's gaze darted wildly from side to side, looking for a place for her lover to hide. 'Under the bed!' she gasped. 'Get underneath!'

Otto fell to the floor. Outside there was the sound of Forz's key in the door. Otto flipped the cover out of his face and started to edge himself underneath the low bed-frame, while Walburga threw on a robe.

'*Ouch!*' he yelped as the cocoon-like protrudance knocked against the bed-frame.

'What's the matter?'

'I can't get under. This sodding salami is in the way!' he gasped in horror as the door to the little house squeaked open.

Hurriedly she stuffed her left breast into her gown and hissed. 'The wardrobe . . . Into the wardrobe!'

'Hello, my little bunny-rabbit,' Forz was cooing from the living-room. 'Where's my little bunny-rabbit! Are we playing games again, cheetah?'

Madly Otto flung his trousers in front of the absurd encumbrance and pushed by her to burrow into the clothes that stank of moth-balls and sweat, pulling them in front of him and whispering urgently. 'In God's name close the door—'

Next instant he wished he had not made the suggestion as the door slapped against the erect cocoon and he bit back his cry of agonized pain just in time. '*Mensch*, what the hell are you trying to do, Walburga? Cut off my shitting salami!'

'I can't close the door!' she hissed in horror. 'It sticks out. I could push, if you—'

Bent double, Otto hushed from the wardrobe. 'Not on your life!' he cried. 'You've got to keep him busy while I sneak out.'

'Yoo-hoo . . . yoo-hoo!' Sergeant Forz was hollering outside, his voice high and expectant like some operette-tenor in an absurd piece by Lehar. 'Where's my little, snuggy-pussy hiding her pretty little self now . . . Yoo-hoo . . .'

'But what can I do?' she cried, wringing her hands in despair. 'There's no other way but the front door.'

Otto made a quick decision. 'Get out there. You got the pants off'f me quick enough. See you do the same for him. Once he's on the job – on that couch of yours – I'll slip by.'

She pouted her bottom lip. 'But that would be indecent,' she said. 'You'll see him . . . doing *it* when you pass.' She shook her head with sudden stubbornness. 'I'd rather he'd find out, than that.'

Otto swallowed the angry retort back just in time, his mind racing wildly. 'No I won't,' he said desperately. 'When I go by, I'll keep my eyes closed.'

'Promise!'

'Promise.'

'Good, then I'll do it.'

'Thank God!' Otto breathed weakly, feeling his legs threatening to give way beneath him at any moment. 'Off you go . . . For God's sake before he comes blundering in here!'

She went.

Tensely, Otto waited, trying to tug on his pants, but finding the white cocoon made any attempt to close the flies impossible, heart thudding, ear pressed to the door expectantly.

Then he heard Forz's cry of delight and the sound of a big paw slapping a naked bottom. Otto whispered the first prayer he had made since he had been kicked out of his confirmation class at the age of fourteen.

A minute or two passed with leaden slowness. There was the sound of a heavy object dropping to the floor and then a second later, another. Forz had just dropped his dice-beakers. Another minute passed. A grunt of pleasure. He was on the job, Otto, tensed behind the bedroom door told himself. The sudden regular squeaking of rusty springs told him that he was right. He forced himself to count to three and then he began to open the door gingerly.

Walburga was sprawled on the couch, legs raised in the air, with Forz between her white plump thighs, massive bottom naked, field-grey trousers wrapped around his ankles, making intensive grunting noises. Walburga saw him and her face grew stern. With her free hand, she touched her eyes warningly.

Hastily Otto nodded his understanding. One hand holding his trousers, the other searching the room ahead of him like a blind man, he tiptoed to the door, heart racing like a trip-hammer, followed by Walburga's stern gaze and accompanied by the animal grunts now reaching their climax as Forz began to win that age-old race.

Five minutes later he was seated in the cover of a grove of thick pines, cautiously picking at the tight bandage with his pocket-knife, the sweat standing out on his forehead in thick pearls, making little yelping sounds every time he nicked himself, swearing all the time that this was the last game he would play with Walburga Forz, the very last. In the end it took him nearly an hour and half to remove the damn thing . . .

That night two things of disparate importance took place. Hitler's troops crossed into Poland and started

World War Two; and Otto Stahl volunteered to accept any outside job that Sergeant Forz found fit to give him.

Forz, relaxed and generous after the incident on the couch that afternoon, didn't object. 'Can't take it, eh, Stahl? The little woman's too much for you, eh?'

Numbly Otto nodded.

Forz beamed. 'All right, you smart-arsed Berliner. I can't say that I like that ugly kisser any more today than when I first saw it. But I feel in a generous mood this evening. Tomorrow morning you report to the thunderboxes. I'll be there to instruct you in the use of the honey-dew wagon.' He threw back his big head and laughed uproariously, as if at some private joke. 'That's gonna come as a surprise for a big city feller like you . . . All right, off you go now. I'll fix it with Frau Forz. I'll tell her that you just couldn't stand the pace.'

'Thank you, Sergeant Forz,' Otto breathed, 'thank you very much!' And there were tears of genuine gratitude in his eyes. *He was saved!*

FOUR

'*The thunderboxes!*' Sergeant Forz, indicated the green-painted wooden structures with the traditional heart, decorated with flowers, carved into each door. 'Got it, arse with ears?'

Otto nodded, saying nothing. Now he had recovered a little from his ordeal at the hands of Walburga Forz and was beginning to wonder just what he had got himself into.

'*The pump!*' Forz barked and pointed to the apparatus to the rear of the latrines, which looked rather like an elongated, old-fashioned water-pump. 'Got it, you cold cucumber?'

Again Otto nodded.

Across the field on the road, a company of *Arbeitsdienst* youths marched, crying at regular intervals the latest victory from the new front in Poland. '*Danzig ist deutsch! . . . Ein Reich, ein Volk, ein Fuhrer!*'

Forz beamed with approval and puffed up his barrel-chest, as if he personally were responsible for the capture of the seaport. '*Now finally the honey-dew wagon*,' he cried as the sound of the singing began to die away. He indicated the long metal barrel, mounted on an ordinary farmer's cart, drawn by an ancient nag, which sagged between the shafts, as if it would fall flat on its face if it were not for their support.

'What is it?' Otto asked for the first time, eyeing the device in bewilderment.

Forz laughed contemptuously. 'I was wondering

when you would ask that, Stahl,' he said. 'We country boys were brought up with such things, but naturally you fine big-city pissers wouldn't know anything about them. Here, look, I'll show you.'

Easily he clambered up on the cart, ignoring the old nag's sigh of despair at the extra weight, and entered the long tube of the pump into the hole in the top of the metal barrel. Deftly he jerked the pump's handle a couple of times.

A stream of thick yellow liquid, obscene and noxious, spurted into the barrel and abruptly the fresh morning air was choked with the stench of faeces.

Otto blanched and staggered back a few paces, as if he had been slapped physically across the face. 'Great God in Heaven,' he blurted out, nauseated. '*Shit!*'

'Exactly, Stahl,' Forz said, dropping from the cart and beaming at him. 'Good honest shit, the waste product of good honest German arses.' His grin increased. 'And from now onwards it will be your task to pump it out of the cesspits of every thunderbox in this area and dump it in the sanitation sector. 'He saw the horrified look on Otto's handsome young face and said insidiously. 'Of course, if you don't like the job, you could go back—'

'No, no,' Otto said hastily, 'I'll take it, Forz! But what do I do with the stuff when I've pumped it out?'

Forz swung round and pointed to the heights which marked the border between Belgium and Germany. 'You see where the secondary road branches off to Schoenberg in Belgie-land? Well, we've got the lime-pits of the sanitation sector up there. It's part of the Chief Engineer's new private hate against the Belgies. He wants us to dump our crap right underneath the garlic-gobblers' dripping noses and give them the full benefit of German culture.'

'I see,' Otto replied.

'Of course you'll be moving out of your present billet into the little shed at the back of the camp,' Forz continued, a malicious grin on his broad red face. 'You understand that?'

'Not really, Forz.'

'Well, do you think anyone would want to sleep in the same room as you after a day's work with the honey-dew cart?' Forz chortled. 'Not on your life! From now onwards, Stahl, you're gonna lead a very lonely existence indeed. But there'll be one consolation.'

'What's that, Forz?' Otto asked unhappily.

'One day when you have kids, and they ask you what you did in the big war. You can say . . . say, *that you shovelled shit for the Fatherland!*' And Sergeant Forz broke out into uproarious laughter, the tears streaming down his face . . .

Thus while in the first days of that September, the German war machine rolled victoriously across Poland, and virtually hourly the fanfares in the radio announced yet another tremendous defeat inflicted on the 'slavic sub-humans', Otto Stahl urged his weary nag back and forth between the camps' various latrines and the 'sanitation sector', a handkerchief tied across his mouth, cotton-wool stuffed in his nostrils, in a vain attempt to keep out that terrible stench, cursing his luck and the all-too-regular bowel movements of his comrades, who seemed to spend virtually all their free time in the thunderboxes.

As Forz had accurately predicted, he had become a very lonely man. When he made his appearance, the other workers made a show of holding their noses and pulling lavatory chains, and would-be comedians made the usual comments about 'attar of roses' and the like. But no one stayed for very long in his presence, in spite of the fact that he scrubbed himself nightly until his skin glowed an angry red and spent half his weekly pay on cheap eau de cologne to spray on his clothes. Occasionally Wurm, the little hunchbacked clerk, would spend a few minutes at the door of the shed in which he now lived, commiserating with him, but finally he, too, would flee, unable to stand the terrible odour any longer. As Otto sadly remarked to the old nag which slept in the other half of the shed, 'Old-timer, we're outcasts, pure and simple, rejected by society.' And the old nag had raised its grizzled head and given a weary nod, as if he agreed with the sentiment.

It was on the fifth day of his new assignment that Otto finally really became aware of the black-uniformed Belgian border-guard, lounging over the red-and-white striped pole which barred the road to the Belgian village of Schoenberg down below in the valley, schako thrust to the back of his shaven head, cigarette seemingly glued to his bottom lip.

'*Bonjour*,' he ventured, reining in the weary spavined horse, glad to have a break from the monotony of his dreary stinking routine, surprised a little that the Belgian had not moved back at the stench coming from the honey-dew wagon.

'*Bonjour*,' the Belgian replied, the cigarette moving up and down with his lip as he spoke. 'Nice load of shit you've got there, Prussian,' he said casually in good German. 'Must be a good *fuder* there.'*

'Could be,' Otto agreed. 'You speak good German.'

'Of course,' the border-guard agreed. 'I was born down there in Schoenberg when it still belonged to you Prussians before 1918 and Versailles.'

'Oh, I see,' Otto absorbed the information, a little amused at the Belgian's use of the word 'Prussian' for German.

'That's my place,' the Belgian pointed to a little red-roofed house about five hundred metres down the road, its walls scarred as if with scabies. 'Got two hectares of land down there. Of course, the old woman has got to work it. I mean I'm too busy up here carrying out my official duties, guarding the frontier. Run off my feet almost, I am.'

'Yes, I suppose so,' Otto agreed with a grin. There probably wouldn't be more than one vehicle a day pass-

* Thousand litres.

ing that particular frontier, he told himself. 'I've never been abroad,' he said. 'Is it any different over there in Belgium?'

The Belgian studied him with eyes that had suddenly narrowed cunningly. 'You'd like to have a look?'

'Well, yes,' Otto said hesitantly. 'But I've got to get rid of this stuff or my boss'll go up the wall.'

'Bring it with you,' the border-guard said eagerly. 'You can dump it at my place. The Old Lady would be glad of that good Prussian shit. I mean horseshit is damn dear these days.'

Otto flung a look to left and right. The wooded, hilly Eifel countryside seemed devoid of human beings. 'All right, I will at that!'

One minute later the pole had been raised and the old nag was plodding its way wearily down the road towards the border-guard's farm and for the first time in his twenty-odd years, Otto Stahl was abroad.

But the surprises did not end there.

After a bottle of *Stella Artois*, the fizzy weak Belgian beer, and several of the *Belga* cigarettes which his new acquaintance Emil Lejeune offered him as they sat there on the bench outside the door watching Madame Lejeune busily spread the nauseating effluence on the land, raking it among the plants, up to the tops of her wooden shoes in the stinking stuff, as if her very life depended upon it, Lejeune called to her, 'All right, woman, don't idle there! Into the kitchen and give our Prussian friend a little recompense in return for his kind gift.'

'Yes, husband,' Madame Lejeune said dutifully. She dropped her rake and stamped into the kitchen to return with the 'recompense' clutched to her massive bosom in big red paws, their skin like emery paper. 'A wheel,' she said, handing a startled Otto a typical round loaf of the area. 'Our own air-dried Ardennes bacon, and this.' She gave the young man a toothless smile and handed across a package which gave off an odour that was excitingly familiar, yet somehow not easy to identify immediately.

'What is it?' he stuttered.

'Why coffee, Prussian,' she said. 'Bean coffee, half a kilo to be exact.'

'Real bean coffee!' Otto exclaimed. 'Why there has been no bean coffee on sale in the Reich since 1937! All we get is ersatz, made of acorns and the like.'

'We've got plenty of it over here,' the farmwoman said, 'Come on, now tuck it under your seat so that the customs-men don't see it.' She winked knowingly at her husband, who grinned back at her.

'But bean coffee's worth a small fortune over in the Reich!' Otto protested. 'At least thirty reichsmark a kilo.'

'*Das ist egal*,' the big woman said. 'It's worth it for us. You can't get that kind of good Prussian crap over here these days. It's yours. Do with it what you wish.'

Five minutes later as Lejeune raised the pole to allow him to pass back into Germany, he said, 'If you've got any more of that stuff, Prussian, I think I could find you plenty of buyers.'

'*Buyers?*'

Emil Lejeune winked solemnly. 'We little men have to make the most of what we've got, Prussian. With luck you can even make chocolate out of shit.' And with that enigmatic remark, he resumed his old position on the pole, cigarette glued to his bottom lip.

FIVE

Thus young Otto Stahl entered upon a new career – of short duration admittedly – but one which was highly lucrative: purveyor of good German manure to the eager, small farmers of the Eastern Canton of St Vith, Belgium.

Business ran splendidly. Three times a day he would guide his weary old horse up to the little border post. There with Emil's help, it would be hastily exchanged for one of the Belgian's own sturdy flemings. Then, while Madame Lejeune guarded the Belgian frontier on behalf of his Majesty Leopold II, King of All Belgians, the two of them would be off at the gallop, the honeydew cart flying behind the fleming, to deliver their wares to the many hamlets that dotted the road between St Vith and Losheim. There, peasant farmers awaited them, bean coffee already bundled up in anticipation, eager to receive their consignment of manure, the like of which their worn-out hill farms had not seen these many years.

Profits were split, it went without saying. After all Emil arranged the contracts and supplied the horse. All the same within a week he had collected some thirty kilograms of bean coffee, hidden in the old nag's feed box, a small fortune at the day's blackmarket prices. By the end of the second week, the feed bin bulged with over seventy kilos of the precious beans and Otto realised that he needed a business agent to get rid of the stuff for him: he couldn't keep accumulating it in this manner. Someone would surely stumble across it sooner or later. Besides it would be too dangerous to unload the coffee in the local area. The locals had no money anyway. As Sergeant Forz often proclaimed contemptuously, 'This lot of half-frogs ain't even got a pot to piss in – they're so poor!'

In the end he decided he must take Wurm, the little hunchbacked clerk, into his confidence, when he ventured over to Otto's shed to chat warily for a few minutes.

'You go to Aachen every Thursday to collect the men's weekly wages for the Friday pay-day, don't you, Wurm?' he asked casually as the two of them sat there smoking reflectively, while across in the billets a triumphant radio announcer was shrilling the great news that Warsaw, the Polish capital, had finally surrendered to the Greater German Army.

'Yes,' Wurm answered, puffing at his little clay-pipe in an attempt to ward off the worse of the stench that came from Otto's direction. 'Why do you ask?'

Otto replied to his question with one of his own. 'How do you get to Aachen – by the local train?'

'No, the Fart-Cannon is magnanimous enough to allow me to take the company truck. After all, I do bring back with me on average five hundred marks or more a week, you know.'

'Little Fish!' Otto said, taking the plunge.

Wurm's curiosity was aroused. 'What do you mean – little fish?'

'What I said. I've got a little project, if you're interested.' He lowered his voice. 'There'll be money in it for you, a lot of money. Surely you're not happy with the kind of peanuts they pay us in this place? You can't get fat on that, Wurm.'

Slowly, his bespectacled face thoughtful, Wurm nodded his agreement.

'Yes, you're right.'

'Of course, I'm right,' Otto urged.

'You know,' Wurm said, lowering his eyes as if he were a little afraid to look the other man in the face, 'that I have certain physical disadvantages. I'm not handsome like you – and I've got this damn hump on my back.'

Now it was Otto's turn to lower his eyes in embarrassment. 'I never had anyone who . . . loved me. You see my parents died when I was a baby and I was brought up by the nuns in a church orphanage in Aachen. That is until I met Gerda.'

'Gerda?' Otto echoed, not wanting to hear any more confessions from the little cripple.

'Yes, my girl,' the hunchback smiled at him. 'I mean, I know she isn't pretty with her cross-eyes and her withered arm.' Otto heard himself muttering that beauty wasn't just skin-deep and feeling a hypocrite for doing so.

'But she loves me and I love her. So we're trying to save a little money to buy a cottage if they'll let us get married. The laws of hereditary diseases you know? My back and her arm.'

Otto nodded his understanding. 'Could be just an accident at birth. Just because you've got a little – er – physical defect, it doesn't mean that your kids will inherit the same thing.'

'That's what we always say,' the hunchback clutched the pathetic straw almost greedily.

'Well, then,' Otto said swiftly, not wanting to hear any more of his cross-eyed Gerda with her withered arm, 'here's your chance to earn the money you need for a down-payment.'

'All right, I'll do it,' Wurm said with new determination. 'What is it?'

'Well, you see, I've come into possession of a lot of real, genuine coffee beans from a source that I am not allowed to divulge to you. Now I want someone to act as my agent on the Aachen blackmarket and Wurm, I think you are *that* man. Well, what do you say?'

Wurm stretched out his skinny little clerk's paw, jaw

hardening like some heroic character in an UFA adventure movie. 'Stahl, I'm your man!'

If he hadn't been so pathetic, Otto could have laughed in his ugly bespectacled face . . .

'You're getting a gut, Wurm,' Sergeant Forz grunted, as the little clerk came through the door carrying a steaming cup of coffee.

The Sergeant sat at his desk, booted feet resting in the 'in' tray, cheap cigar in his mouth, the coffee pot steaming on the pot-bellied stove behind him, reading the front page of the Nazi *Westdeutsche Allgemeine*, with its account of the final dismemberment of a defeated Poland by the two new allies Russia and Germany. 'Don't yer know that a good cock never gets fat,' he added when the clerk didn't answer, and chuckled. 'But then no woman in her right mind would want a little cripple like you, would she?'

'I suppose so, sergeant,' Wurm said, lowering his gaze so that the big NCO would not see the look of hate and triumph in his eyes. What did the ugly fart-cannon know, he asked himself. Hadn't Gerda allowed him to make love to her in the back of the truck last Thursday after he had given her, for the second time, two hundred reichsmarks, his share of the money he had made on Aachen's blackmarket selling Otto's coffee?

'What time are you off?' Forz asked.

'As soon as I finish my coffee, sergeant.'

'No time for that. I want the truck back here by four so that you can get straight on filling the wage packets for tomorrow.'

Wurm put down his coffee. 'As you wish.'

'And don't forget my cigars, Wurm, or I'll have your arse.'

'Yes, Sergeant,' Wurm replied dutifully. 'Twenty, wasn't it?'

Forz nodded, his gaze fixed on his newspaper once more.

'Right, Sergeant, that'll be two marks.' Wurm held out his little hand for the money.

Forz pretended to be engrossed in his newspaper.

Wurm gave a little shrug and slinging his pack containing the precious coffee beans went out, trying not to hear Forz's low laugh of contempt as he did so.

'Stupid little crippled bastard,' Forz said to himself as the truck started up outside. 'Still wet behind the spoons. Falls for the same old trick every Thursday, he does.' He sighed and made himself more comfortable at his desk. It was going to be a nice easy day and at dinnertime there might be more than a good strong pea soup waiting for him back home. For a few minutes he savoured the memories of that delightful, if surprising incident on the couch of three weeks ago before gradually he started to become aware of the strange, exotic odour.

He sat up and sniffed hard. What was it? He looked at his cheap cigar. It had gone out. The smell didn't come from that source. He frowned and a little intrigued rose to his feet heavily to stare around the office.

There seemed nothing out of the ordinary. His narrow animal brow wrinkled in bewilderment. Like a bloodhound sniffing out its prey, he stamped around the office, his flared, hairy nostrils twitching as he tried to locate the source of the strange odour.

And then he had it. It came from the little cripple's still steaming coffee cup!

He lifted up the chipped, cheap cup and sniffed hesitantly.

By God, he told himself, it did smell like the real thing. He wiped his lips with one sweep of his hairy paw and took a tentative sip, and then another, and another. Suddenly his bushy eyebrows slid up his forehead like twin lifts with astonishment. *It was the real thing!* In one gulp he drained the rest of the brown liquid. There was no denying it. The little cripple Wurm had been drinking real bean coffee!

Suddenly, as if overcome by the discovery, Forz

slumped down into his chair, his mind racing, his newspaper forgotten now. What was Wurm up to? he asked himself. Wurm, whose weekly wage was all of forty marks, was drinking real bean coffee which, even if one could find a black marketeer selling the precious stuff, cost at least thirty reichsmark a kilo, a sum impossible for that little crippled shit to raise.

He was getting fat too, in spite of the fact that he, Forz, kept him on the move six days a week. It couldn't be the camp grub either. Those greedy bastards of kitchen bulls wouldn't give you the dirt from beneath their nails and nobody could grow a gut on the watery horse-meat soups and greasy soya-bean hashes they dished out.

Forz rubbed his big black chin, only half-hearing the rasp of the stubble. Wurm was getting money from somewhere, lots of it! But from where?

Forz pondered that question for a very long time, his slow mind coming up with answer after answer which he dismissed almost as soon as it came to him. And then he had it with the startling clarity of a sudden vision.

'Of course,' he cried out loud. 'Of course it has to be that!' Abruptly he experienced the delightful mental picture of the promotion this discovery would bring him, perhaps even a medal. Walburga would be as proud of him again as she had been the day they had married and in spite of the fact that four comrades had been necessary to carry his drunken body into the bridal chamber, she had been very willing and appreciative once he had come to again.

Sergeant Forz hesitated no longer. With a sausage-like forefinger that trembled slightly with barely controlled excitement he dialled the secret Aachen number, which had been given to him specifically for just such cases, though he had never expected he would ever have occasion to use it.

Impatiently he waited for the other party to come through.

Finally a gruff, bored, masculine voice rasped,

'Geheime Staatspolizei, Dienststelle Aachen.'

'Gestapo?' he said somewhat stupidly.

'No, we're the home for fallen mothers,' the gruff voice snarled. 'I've just said we are, you idiot!'

'Sorry, sorry,' Forz said hastily. 'Sergeant Forz here, Westwall, Sector Four . . . I'm afraid I'm a bit excited.'

'Well, don't have an orgasm, Sergeant,' the Gestapo man replied without any particular interest. 'Where's the fire? What is it? Cough it up!'

Sergeant Forz drew a deep breath, his mind full of medals and naked women. 'Sir,' he said firmly, 'I would like to report a case . . . a case of espionage . . .'

SIX

Cautiously the little hunchback parked the battered old engineers' truck behind the huge, domed cathedral which housed the throne of the great Charlemagne himself, the emperor who had made this his imperial city over a thousand years before. Not that such things interested Wurm, who had been brought up in Aachen. Hunchbacked orphans with weak eyes usually have little time for glory and history; they are much too humble and concerned with simple survival.

He pulled the brake and turned off the engine to turn to Gerda, sitting in the cab next to him. Patting her skinny knee, encased in the thick woollen stockings she knitted herself in her sparse off-duty time as a scullery-maid in the home of one of Aachen's textile manufacturers, he said, 'Now, Gerda, I don't want you to move away from the truck. You just watch the wages under the seat. Don't open the door to anyone but me. Do you understand?'

'No I won't open the door, Klaus. And I won't leave the truck too,' she said in that slow illogical manner of hers and gave him a loving, cross-eyed look.

He smiled back at her and wished again she would not always let her tongue hang out of the corner of her slack mouth as though she were an idiot. These days the Nazi authorities were quick enough to whip anyone who looked slightly mental into one of those discreet secluded country 'sanitoria', from which they mostly returned to their loved ones inside an urn with the polite noncommittal statement that 'Patient X or Y' had died unexpectedly of an infectious disease which had 'necessitated immediate cremation'. Still, he could never be angry with Gerda in spite of her defects. She was always so loving, humble and grateful – and she had let him make love to her thirty minutes ago in the back of the truck in Aachen's well-wooded *Staatsforst*. So he slung his pack, containing the precious coffee beans, flashed her another smile and with a soft '*bis bald*' was gone.

The Aachen blackmarket, centred in the narrow cobbled medieval streets around the great romanesque cathedral, was in 1939 only a shadow of the booming business centre it would become in 1944–5 when Otto Stahl was the uncrowned king of the illegal border trade. Yet due to the fact that it was still only a tram-ride from Aachen to those lands of plenty, Belgium and Holland, which were not affected by the severe restrictions placed on luxuries by a National Socialist Germany whose motto was 'guns before butter', the illicit market-place thrived.

There were Jews, for once wearing the yellow star of David willingly as a signal to the dealers that they were there to do business, wanting to trade their gold and jewels for foreign currency to take with them for the long illegal journey to Palestine. By now most of them knew that just before the border the police would give them a large dose of castor oil to ensure that they did not smuggle out any such valuables in their stomachs. Foreign currency could be smuggled out to Holland or Belgium by means of sending a letter to onself poste restante Verviers, Liège or Maastricht.

There were hard-pressed housewives, eager to find good Dutch butter without which no confirmation, birthday, or wedding celebration could be a success; for who had ever heard of a German party without a belly-filling selection of *puffers* and *torten*?

There were shabby men in blue overalls, taking precious time off work, in order to find an inner-tube or even a tyre to replace yet another torn synthetic product from Buna so that they could get to the factory the next morning on their bikes or motorbikes.

And then there were the dealers, those flashy creatures from both sides of the border with their ringed fingers and greased hair who dominated the market, making it all possible by their liberal backhanders to the fat-bellied green-uniformed *Schupos* who never seemed to interfere with the illegal trade right in the heart of the ancient imperial city, and their generous donations to the uniformed 'Winter Help' collectors, who were everywhere in that tight mass of eager, desperate, hopeful, pessimistic people.*

Slowly the little hunchback, not minding the buffeting he was receiving from the throng, made his way around the cathedral for the third time, eyeing the dealers and making his assessment of the one who might be financially capable of taking his coffee in one go and still paying him a suitable price.

So, thus occupied, fully immersed in his task, he did not realise he was being followed until it was too late and the two heavy-set men in the long green leathercoats and with their dark felt hats pulled low over their brows were right behind him.

'*Herr* Wurm?' a deep polite voice asked.

He turned round startled, and his heart sank as he recognised them for what they were, even before the older of the two pulled the medal badge from inside his pocket and whispered softly so the people nearby could not hear, '*Geheime Staatspolizei.*'

Gestapo! The frightening thought flashed through Wurm's mind. They knew all about the smuggled coffee. Panicked beyond all reason, Wurm thrust out his puny clerk's hand.

* Money collected by the Party to distribute to poor people in the winter.

The older Gestapo man was caught completely by surprise. He staggered against the railings, dragging his assistant with him. Next moment Wurm was off at a crazy gallop, pelting down the narrow lane which led to the cathedral, the rucksack bouncing up and down on his crooked shoulders, while the older official fought to tug his pistol out of his pocket.

His assistant was quicker off the mark. In an instant he whipped out his Walther and standing as if on a police training range, while the scared civilians scattered wildly on both sides, he called as Gestapo Regulations prescribed, '*Stehenblieben, oder ich schiesse!*'

Wurm heard the words, but they meant nothing to him in his unreasoning fear. He kept on running.

The assistant's jaw hardened.

'Warning shot in the air first,' the older man, still struggling to free his pistol, cried in red-faced anger. '*In the air!*'

But the other man was not listening. His whole being was concentrated on the spot just below the running man's rucksack. He gave a little grunt, and pressed the trigger.

The Walther erupted in his fist. A woman screamed and the dealers started to bolt for cover, wondering what had gone wrong. Had they not been generous enough with the bribes to the Gestapo?

Wurm staggered. A great wave of almost unbearable pain swept through his body. For one long moment he stood there, too shocked to move, all breath knocked from his lungs by that tremendous impact. Then he remembered poor Gerda waiting for him in the truck. He started to stagger forward again, reeling from side to side of the dark alley like a drunken man, mumbling her name again and again.

The assistant didn't hesitate. He pressed the trigger once more. The second bullet struck the rucksack in the very same instant that his superior knocked the pistol out of his hand with an angry, 'What in God's name do you think you're doing, man? This is not the Wild West.

This is Aachen . . . Come on, after him!'

Together the two Gestapo officials started to run heavily after the cripple, their leather coats creaking audibly as they did so, crunching over the dark beans which a dying Wurm was leaving in a trail behind him as he tried to reach his Gerda before it was too late.

He reached the corner. There was the truck. Gerda was staring at him through the glass, cross-eyes wide with horror. 'It's all right, Gerda . . . all right,' he tried to say. But the words wouldn't come; his mouth was too full of blood. He reached out his little hand. Like a child parodying an adult, Gerda did the same. 'That's right,' he said to himself happily, the red mist in front of his eyes growing ever thicker. 'Touch my—' Abruptly his knees gave way completely. He slammed to the floor face-first, his glasses shattering, something which made him feel infinitely sad for a fleeting second for a reason he couldn't quite comprehend. Then his head lolled to one side and he was dead.

'Poor little crippled shit,' the older Gestapo man said, turning over the dead clerk with the toe of his boot. 'All for the sake of a couple of kilos of bean coffee.'

'A blackmarket parasite, all the same,' his assistant said. The other man looked at him. 'We're all parasites, Schmitz,' he sneered. 'Didn't you know that?'

Schmitz flushed and wondered whether one could denounce a Gestapo-man to the Gestapo. Aloud he said, 'What now, sir?'

'You'd better get up to that labour camp and see where the cripple was getting the stuff from. And Schmitz.'

'Sir?'

'Give that big-mouthed Army shit who denounced him a right royal rocket from me. Understood?'

'Verstanden Herr Oberkommissar!'

Twenty-four hours later *Gestapo-Kommissar* Schmitz arrested Otto Stahl.

SEVEN

The heavy-set judge strode resolutely into the court, his choleric, crazy man's eyes bulging from a coarse, heavy face, his hard jaw and cheek criss-crossed with scars from his student duelling days. Without ceremony he plumped himself in the largest of the three chairs set on the dias decorated with the swastika flag and flung back his silken robe with an imperious gesture to reveal the black uniform of an officer of the *Allgemeine SS** beneath.

A little hesitantly, as if they wondered whether they ought to ask for permission first, his two assistant judges stole into their places on either side of him.

Behind the prisoner and his guard, the handful of spectators shuffled their feet and sat down too. At Otto's side, his fat warder Heinz tugged the handcuff-chain and whispered, 'All right, lad, you can rest your weight too now.'

Otto sat down and stared back at the Chief Judge boldly, though he had never felt less brave than he did at that moment. He knew the type well enough. He was one of the new National Socialist judges: brutal, harsh, uncontrolled men, who shouted a great deal and hammered on their desks with their fists, enjoying the almost limitless new power given to them by the autocratic Third Reich. As his mother, the Witch, who had been up before them more than once in Berlin in these

* General SS.

last few years, was wont to comment: 'That kind'll say "off with his turnip" as quick as yer average husband says to his old woman on Saturday night after a couple of beers – "off with yer knickers"!'

For a few minutes, the Chief Judge made a play of searching through the pile of papers before him on his desk, though he didn't take his hard-eyed, ruthless gaze off Otto's pale tense face for one instant. Then finally he was ready.

'Accused!' he barked in a high-pitched, surprisingly feminine voice.

Heinz dug Otto in the ribs and rose hastily to his feet himself, dragging the prisoner with him by the chain that linked their wrists together. Otto stood there and waited, feeling very exposed and lonely.

'Accused,' the Chief Judge rasped, glancing down at his papers now, 'you have to answer to the following charges. One, you stole government property, namely from Sector Four of the so-called . . . er . . . *Westwall*. Two, you did, knowing well that this was government property, sell the same property illegally to a citizen of a foreign country in that same foreign country. Three, you journeyed abroad without the legal and proper exit-visa. Four, in recompense for your illegally sold stolen property in a foreign country, you imported into the Third Reich coffee illegally and sold it, also illegally, on the blackmarket in the city of Aachen.' The Chief Judge cleared his throat. 'Fifth, it might well have been possible from the quantity of the property you stole for agents of a foreign power, known to be unfriendly to our Fatherland, to have made some estimate of the number of our brave soldiers manning the so-called – er Westwall.' The Chief Judge took a quick drink of water from the glass in front of him. 'Accused, how do you plead – guilty or not guilty?' The man's bulging eyes bore into Otto, who stood there a little helplessly, overwhelmed by the apparent magnitude of his crimes.

'But sir,' Otto stuttered finally, 'I mean it was only sh—'

'How do you plead, Accused?' the Chief Judge interrupted him brutally.

'And it wasn't really abroad, only down the road.'

The Chief Judge's face flushed a frightening crimson and his eyes seemed about to explode out of his head. '*How do you plead?*' he screamed, foam flecking the corners of his mouth.

'Not guilty, sir,' Otto answered miserably, knowing that he was not going to be given a chance in this particular 'People's Court'.

He slumped into his seat as the Chief Judge dismissed him and nodded to the waiting prosecutor, a fat oily balding lawyer, who had been rubbing his fat paws together all the while the Chief Judge had spoken, as if he were warming them on the other man's fiery words. '*Herr Kollege, Sie haben das Wort.*' Otto let his shaven head fall and the flood of words descend upon him, not caring much now, knowing that his fate was probably already sealed.

'Criminal audacity to steal valuable Reich property . . . transport illegally across the Belgian frontier using government conveyances . . . purchased by a large number of Belgian nationals who might well have been working for French or British intelligence . . . possibly have gained valuable information . . . about our glorious Wehrmacht and our latest fortifications, so generously provided by our Fuhrer Adolf Hitler . . .'

On and on the legal jargon went and in the end Otto whispered in disgust to Heinz, 'You'd think I'd stolen the Prussian crown jewels or something, Corporal . . . After all, it was only shit!'

'Silence, Accused!' the Chief Judge rasped.

Otto gave up.

The defending lawyer, provided by the Poor Law Regulations, a nervous bespectacled young Catholic, whose sole claim to legal fame would be that in late 1944 he challenged the notorious Justice Freisler on a legal point at the great Assassination Plot Trials* before Freisler had him sentenced to be garrotted to death – slowly, did his best. He attempted to minimise the offence by trying to explain the exact nature of the 'Reich property' which had been stolen.

He didn't get far in the attempt. After giving the pale-faced young Catholic the full benefit of his invective and sarcasm, the Chief Judge had cried as if he were before some film court in one of those melodramatic UFA trial movies, 'Germany is fighting for its very life. We must be self-sufficient. Everything that has to be imported costs the Reich precious foreign currency. Has not Reich Marshal Goering stated time and time again that it is guns before butter for us? Has not the Fuhrer himself said that the humble German rhubarb is better than the costly decadent foreign lemon?' He raised his index finger and thrust up his jaw like the Fuhrer addressing a million-strong audience at the annual Party Rally in Nuremburg. 'That humble manure, as you deign to call it, Mr Defender, could have been used to cultivate German food, saving valuable foreign monies needed now to import artificial products.' He flung his head from side to side, like a cow trying to shake off flies on a hot summer's day, spittle everywhere. 'That shit, as you have seen fit to name the stolen property . . . *that shit . . . could have filled German bellies!*' He glared at the embarrassed young lawyer, who lowered his gaze in defeat.

At 11.30 that September morning as the prosecuting lawyer was half through his final summing-up, the Chief Judge started to look at his gold watch with ever-increasing frequency, as if he wanted the fat lawyer to get it over with. Otto saw the looks and told himself that

* Chief Judge and prosecutor of those accused of having attempted to murder Hitler in July 1944.

all of them had made up their minds. He hadn't a chance. Now it was only a question of just how high his sentence would be. For a few moments Otto reflected on fate's quirks; how poor old Wurm had been shot to death for a few kilos of coffee; and how he was going to land behind bars for, probably, several long years, just on account of a little human manure. There seemed little logic or reason to it.

At 11.45, the Chief Justice had apparently had enough, for he suddenly interrupted the prosecutor with a curt, '*Genug!* Court will be recessed till fourteen hundred hours when sentence will be passed.' He stood up abruptly and put his square judge's cap on. The prosecutor stopped immediately and everyone rose to his feet. In a great hurry the Chief Judge bolted for the door, undoing his robe as he did so, followed by his two assistants.

Next to a miserable Otto, Heinz farted with relief. 'Can't get to the trough quick enough that one,' he commented. 'Come twelve o'clock and dinnertime and he'd sentence Christ to the Cross in double-quick time so that he wouldn't be late for his sodding grub!'

Otto nodded and turned to watch the handful of spectators file out, just in time to catch a quick glimpse of a strange figure pose for an instant at the door and survey him with eyes that gleamed white like hard-boiled eggs before placing a large, broad-brimmed black hat of the kind favoured by the older generation of German actors on his silver-grey hair with a theatrical gesture and vanishing.

Otto frowned and then dismissed the spectator as Heinz grunted, 'Come on, old son, let's get back to the cells. I've ordered us sauer-kraut and pig's knuckle and it would be a pity to let it get cold.'

'What do you think?' Otto asked, toying with the great mound of gleaming pink meat surrounded by a marsh of cooling sauer-kraut.

Heinz wiped ends of cabbage from his moustache and levered a piece of meat from his teeth with his thumbnail. 'You ain't eaten much, son,' he commented and raised, 'What do I think – about what?'

'What I'll get?'

'It all depends on what the cheesehands serve him in the way of grub,' Heinz answered and belched.

'You mean the Chief Judge is in Holland?' Otto said incredulously.

'Of course,' Heinz said easily. 'You don't think big animals like that eat our common German grub. Every time he comes down here from Dusseldorf for a trial, he's off like a shot at dinnertime over the Dutch border at Vaals to fill his face with cheesehead grub.'

'But where does he get his visa from . . . and foreign currency as well?' Otto said hotly.

Heinz smiled at the young man's outraged look benignly. 'I thought you was from the big city, son? You should know how these things are. There's one law for the rich and one for the poor – us.'

'And he's gonna give me years behind Swedish curtains for selling a load of shit over the border!' Otto moaned.

Heinz clapped him on the shoulder. 'Don't think about it, lad. Just get yer biters into that pig's knuckle. Where you're going after this afternoon, they only serve you grub like that the day before the executioner lops off yer turnip . . .'

At 1.50, his pig's knuckle still only half-eaten, Otto began to get uneasy. Two o'clock came. No summons to attend the court. 2.30 came and went. 'Perhaps, his nibs has gone and choked on a bone of one of them fancy carp-fish he likes to eat,' Heinz commented and Otto could see that he, too, was puzzled by the fact that they were still waiting.

When at three o'clock they had still not been summoned, Heinz decided to go and find out what was happening up above in the court-room. He went and did not return.

Another thirty minutes passed and by now Otto was pacing the narrow cell nervously and urinating ever more frequently into the enamel bucket in the corner. It was while he was thus occupied that there was a soft tap on the door of his cell, Otto swung round, penis still in his hand, mouth open stupidly.

'May I come in?' a cultivated voice asked quietly.

Otto was too surprised to answer the next instant, the key turned in the door. It creaked opened to reveal the big stranger in the broad-brimmed hat and ankle-length cloak who he had glimpsed leaving the court at midday. His white eyes fell on Otto's hand holding his penis and he said conversationally, 'Passing the time away, I see, Herr Stahl. As a young man, I used to find it a great comfort too.'

Angrily, going red in spite of himself, Otto stuffed the organ back into his trousers. 'No, I was just taking a piss,' he snorted.

The stranger smiled but said nothing and for a few moments they stared at each other in silence.

Otto saw a flamboyant, middle-aged man with his grey hair a little too long, who made even the business of standing still seem somehow theatrical, and who smelled of expensive perfume. The stranger saw a keen-eyed, intelligent young man with a handsome determined face, which, although it had a 'slight working-class hang' (as he phrased it to himself) about it, still could mix with every class and type without causing comment.

'Stahl, eh,' the stranger broke the silence finally, '*nomen est omen*, what?'

'I seem to have heard that particular Latin phrase before,' Otto said sourly.

The stranger smiled winningly. 'Of course, I'm sure you have. Truth is a thing which is hard and dangerous – like steel,' he said mysteriously.

In years to come Otto would learn that his boss would

always have some such mysterious saying at the ready until one day in early 1945, the Gestapo hangman put an end to those ready phrases – with a short length of thin chicken wire at Flossenberg Concentration Camp.

'But I am forgetting my *knigge**. Let me introduce myself, my dear Stahl,' the stranger swept off his broad-brimmed hat and bowed solemnly like an actor in an eighteenth century costume drama. 'Dr Rantzau, alias William B. Harper, Mynheer van Elst, Monsieur Le Comte de deux Eglises, Senor Angelo, Xavier de Dos Santos . . .'

Otto regarded him in open-mouthed amazement as he reeled off the long list of foreign names, changing his accent to fit each new one, stumbling a little with his Russian alias until finally choking for breath, he gasped, 'In truth, all aliases for *Graf* von der Weide, my humble self, presently code-named 'Meadow'. English, you know?' He beamed at an absolutely bewildered Otto, 'I wonder now that introductions have been made, if I could sit down, Otto? You don't mind if I call you Otto, do you, my dear chap? Time is a too precious commodity to waste on the trivia of formality, don't you think?'

Speechless, Otto waved his hand at the latrine bucket and then when he saw the sudden worried look on the Count's fleshly handsome, middle-aged face, he indicated the cot hurriedly.

The Count sat down on the hard bench and sighed gratefully. He smoothed a pale, carefully manicured hand across his long grey hair and said, 'Already the first snow has fallen, as you can see. One tires readily these days.'

'Yes, yes,' Otto agreed, hardly knowing what he was agreeing to.

The Count took out a little box of gold, decorated with small, fire-red rubies. 'You care for a pinch?' he enquired.

'A pinch?' Otto echoed stupidly.

* The German form of etiquette.

'Snuff. One of my many vices.'

Hastily Otto shook his head and watched how, in that theatrical manner of his, the Count went through the ritual of applying delicate pinches of snuff to each nostril and then, when he had sneezed and his eyes were full of tears, he jumped up and stared at his face in the cell's little steel shaving mirror; as if he saw there a tragic but romantic figure: the face of a man of destiny, its pallor coming from the coldness of fate itself.

Suddenly the Count smiled and his man-of-destiny face vanished immediately. 'I look at myself often in mirrors and shop windows,' he said. 'I sometimes think there is a streak of the homosexual in me, though I have always been very much inclined towards the ladies. They say, don't they, those clever Jewish doctors from Vienna, that we all have elements of both sexes in us, though I suppose in this particular place one shouldn't express that kind of sentiment too loudly, what? He gave a melodramatic shudder.

'Now Otto, why am I here?' he said, his voice businesslike at last. 'I am sure you are asking yourself that question?'

'Yes, I am,' Otto said, finally recovering from the shock of meeting this strange, overwhelming aristocrat.

'Well, I can't tell everything at once. After all, caution is the mother of the china cabinet, as they say. But in essence I am here to make you a proposition.'

'A proposition?'

'Yes, I am offering you a chance to get out of this place before that monster of a judge has his way with you. God knows what he would do with you, if you had committed a real crime? I shudder at the very thought! At all events, he's talking of ten years' hard labour for you, in spite of Mynheer de Smits's best culinary efforts in Vaals which, according to my informant has already cost the German state one hundred reichsmarks of illegal Dutch guilders.'

'Ten years for a heap of shit,' Otto stuttered wildly, 'And he spends a small fortune . . .'

The Count smiled, 'Don't take on, old chap. Be above it. Everything is relative, you know, as that Jewish fellow Einstein maintains. Tut-tut,' he shook his head in mock annoyance. 'I really have a thing about the Hebrews this afternoon. I must be more careful, I really must.'

'The proposition?' Otto interrupted him.

'Oh, yes, the proposition. Well, my dear young friend, it's either ten years in the jute mills or join us.'

'Join you?'

'Yes.'

'But what are you?'

The Count beamed at him. 'I thought everybody in this area knew who old Meadow was? Sorry. We're the *Abwehr*.' He gave the dumbstruck Otto the full benefit of his expensively gold-capped teeth. 'You know, my dear fellow, the spy chappies.'

TWO : OTTO ENTERS THE SECRET SERVICE

'The more I see of men, the more I like animals.'

Otto von Bismarck

'The following morning when the alarm clock sounded its raucous message, Idris fled into those indefinite regions which lie between sleep and wakefulness, unwilling to answer its call. This was territory in which he took refuge whenever a night of drinking lay behind him, and a day of work ahead.'

Andrew Kay, *Bland Street*

ONE

'Pigeon-shit!' Hirsch, the little Jewish instructor, said for the second time and flicked a white spot from his dirty, stained waistcoat. 'Pigeon-shit, that's the best you can use in an emergency.'

Otto sighed. It seemed ever since he had gone out into the world to seek his fortune, he had kept landing in the shit, in both senses of the phrase. Now, apparently, he was in it once more. He made a little gesture of irritation with his pencil.

'No notes, Number Sixty-Nine,' Hirsch said sternly, looking at him over the edge of his nickel-rimmed spectacles. 'Keep everything in your head. First rule of clandestine activity, Sixty-Nine.'

'Yes,' Otto caught himself in time from using Hirsch's own name, though after training was over for the day, everyone used it in the little mess of that remote country house. 'Yes, Number Nine.' 'Right, then let's get on with it. As I was saying – pigeon shit . . .' Otto slumped in his seat with resignation and hoped he wouldn't go to sleep again. Twice this week he had done so during lectures; it was the fault of the very boozy lunches they served at the *Abwehr* training school.

It was a week now since the strange Count, or 'Meadow', as he preferred to be called, had deposited him at the *Abwehr* training school not far from the border town of Duren, where, according to the Count, the Secret Service had a company of its own special commandos, the Brandenburgers. He had been given a Brandenburger uniform himself, though without any badges of rank or unit identification. 'Never let the chaps of the Regular Army catch you outside dressed the way you are,' the Count had warned him seriously. 'They'll see straight away you're no soldier. Spot you for a spy right off.' Suddenly he had laughed and said, 'And in a way they would be right, eh, Otto?' And with that enigmatic statement he had departed, leaving a puzzled Otto to cope with the strnge life of the remote country-house training school – and even stranger individuals who ran it.

There was 'Brass Eggs', for instance, a frail, scented, wavy-haired lieutenant in the Brandenburgers who taught him unarmed combat and who invariably grabbed for his testicles during their staged fights together with the comment, 'brass eggs, always give them the brass eggs, Sixty-Nine.' Twice a weary Otto had spotted him sneaking off up the road that led to Duren, dressed in a tight-fitting sailor's suit with what appeared to be a lady's handbag slung over his skinny arm, and it hadn't taken much imagination to guess what he was up to. By the end of the week he and Brass Eggs were tossing each other all over the coconut matting of the gym like the best of enemies.

'Maps', his map-reading instructor, was yet another of the teachers who seemed to be leading a strange secret life. During the day the big, bluff civilian appeared perfectly normal, a dry, rational individual, whose life centered around contour lines, grid references and compass bearings. But in the evening he changed completely, the confident look vanished from his face to be replaced by a nervous haunted one, as if he were a sorely troubled man. Twice an astonished Otto had come across him on his knees, scrubbing madly at the great wooden steps that led upstairs, the sweat pouring from his face as he dipped his brush in the pail of steaming suds and belaboured the eighteenth century woodwork, as if his very life depended upon it, muttering to himself that 'they' were 'everywhere'. On the second occasion Otto had ventured to ask who 'they' were. Maps had paused for an instant, wiping the sweat off his brow with the back of his wet hand like a charlady might, and had whispered solemnly, ''Fraid I can't tell you, Sixty-Nine. Not at this moment, you understand.' He had jerked his scrubbing brush in the direction of the roof and added, 'They're up there, you know. Listening to every word we say. Must get rid of as many of them as I can.' And with that he had commenced scrubbing furiously once more.

Once Otto had caught a brief glimpse of Maps standing out on the lawn below, clad in gum-boots with a piece of lace curtain wrapped around his head like a beekeeper's veil, but otherwise stark naked in spite of the dawn cold, busily spraying his clothes which were spread out in front of him on the grass with a flit-gun. Otto nicked himself twice shaving that particular morning.

'Slightly peculiar, I suppose,' the Commandant, Major Haase, had agreed reluctantly when Otto had remarked upon Maps' strange behaviour to him. 'But you must understand, Sixty-Nine, that all the staff here are highly gifted individuals.' He had beamed at Otto. 'And they do say that genius is akin to madness, don't they? I mean, look at you, Sixty-Nine.'

Otto had flinched again at the use of his awful code-name and wondered who had bestowed it on him. Somehow he suspected it might have well been Brass Eggs. 'How do you mean, Number One?'

'You seem perfectly sane and rational, in spite of having the Count for your father.'

'What . . . the Count is supposed to be my father?' Otto had exploded.

The major had winked solemnly. 'Never fear, Sixty-Nine, your secret is safe with me.'

Next morning the fat major had taken up Otto's pistol training himself, appearing in the grey uniform of a female Army auxiliary, complete with sling-bag and short skirt which rode up his fat thighs every time he knelt to demonstrate a shot to reveal the salmon-pink straps of an issue garter belt. 'Just one of my disguises, Sixty-Nine,' he had said calmly when Otto's face had revealed his astonishment. 'Not to worry, all in a day's work.'

'Now supposing,' Hirsch, the Jewish instructor in codes and secret-writing, was saying, 'that the agent does not have a tame pigeon at his disposal to obtain our raw material, pigeon-shit, what is he to do, *prego*?'

Hirsch had grown his side-chats long and dyed his hair jet-black to give his Jewish features what he fondly imagined was an Italianate cast; and it was for this same reason that he threw an occasional Italian word into his lectures. Not that Hirsch's Jewishness worried Otto. In this crazy place, he told himself, anything could happen.

'This. *Ecco!*' Hirsch pulled a handful of what appeared to be bird-seed out of his waistcoat pocket, like a magician pulling a rabbit out of his top-hat and beamed at Otto as if he had just achieved something of importance.

Inwardly Otto groaned.

'Sprinkle some of this on your window-sill,' he suited his actions to his words and spread the seed on the table in front of him, making cooing, encouraging noises, as if hesitant pigeons were already approaching the imaginary balcony. 'Park benches are also particularly good for this kind of operation, Sixty-Nine, especially if children are about to provide the agent with cover. *Bambini* make an ideal distraction. Now the collection of the shit presents a few problems but, *pazienza*, there are ways to obtain the vital raw material, once the dear little *paloma* has deposited it right under our noses. All we need is a spoon and . . .'

Otto gave up. He closed his eyes and dozed off, forgetting the production of secret ink from pigeon shit for this particular afternoon.

It was in the third week of his 'training' at that remote country house that Otto learned for the first time why the Count had freed him from the Gestapo's clutches. As usual, Thursday morning's training had commenced with bayonet fighting. Under the command of a burly Regular Army sergeant, he was supposed to be running screaming at a line of sacks filled with sawdust and, suspended from wooden frames, rip his bayonet into them and bellow, 'take that, you swine, right in the guts . . . Buckets of blood, that's what we love, *buckets of blood*!'

'But you said you were going to teach how to kill silently,' he gasped in protest, his face lathered in sweat, after the first run. 'Hell, the way I was shouting, the shitting Hottentots down in Africa could hear me!'

The sergeant tugged at the end of his schnaps-thickened red nose. 'Never does as an NCO says, son, allus does as he does!' he said enigmatically.

'Oh, my aching back,' Otto groaned, 'doesn't anybody in this clapmill speak clear-text! If this goes on much longer, they'll be taking me away in the rubber-wagon. Christ, can't you—'

'Never despair, young friend,' a well-known, fruity voice said calmly.

'Remember, *Lehrjahre sind keine Herrenjahre*.'*

Otto spun round and gasped. Next to him, the sergeant's clay-pipe dropped from his mouth in astonishment and shattered on the ground.

'Holy strawsack,' he choked, 'what is *it*?'

'It' was the Count, three days' growth on his plump face, dressed in a British Army khaki tunic, a bedraggled kilt, with one red-flannel underpant-leg hanging down over his muddy knee. 'Been on a mission to Scottish comrades over there,' the Count explained, indicating the general direction of the French border where Otto knew the British now had an army in the line next to the

* Roughly equivalent to: 'You've got to learn to walk, before you can run'.

French. 'They're nationalist to the man. Should imagine they'll simply drop their weapons when the balloon goes up and join us to fight for Scotland's freedom. They do drink a lot though.' He drew up his wet kilt and arranged his red-flannel underpants while the other two stared at him dumbfounded. 'Unfortunately I ran into a damn SS corporal on the way back. Couldn't convince him I wasn't a woman. I think he'd been drinking. He chased me half a kilometre up the road before I managed to shake him off by wading the River Sauer.' He bent and, twisting the heavy material of the kilt, drained a couple of litres of river-water out of it. 'Still, as Confuscius himself said, "Lady with skirt up can run faster than man with trousers down – hence no rape".' He beamed at Otto winningly.

Otto could do nothing but groan and hold his head in mock anguish.

The Count didn't seem to notice. 'All right, Sergeant, you can cut along now,' he ordered. 'You've done an excellent job with Sixty-Nine here. Congratulations.'

'Thank you, sir.' The NCO flushed red with pleasure and flung the man in the kilt a tremendous salute before departing.

'Done?' Otto echoed, finding his voice for the first time since the Count had made his unexpected and decidedly very strange appearance.

'Yes, my boy,' He put his arm round Otto's shoulders in a paternal manner. 'Just had word from old Father Christmas himself in Berlin. Gertie, the Commandant, passed it straight to me a minute ago. Unusually prompt for her, I must say.'

'But what is it?' Otto exploded, not even daring to ask who old 'Father Christmas' in Berlin was and why the Count referred to Major Haase as 'Gertie'.

'You've got a mission,' the Count answered affably. 'You're off this very afternoon . . . Now I must really change my knickers. They're absolutely soaked.'

TWO

As soon as Otto saw Madame Lejeune he knew instinctively he should not have come; he had been too clever by half. There was obviously something wrong, very seriously wrong. Like most humble people she didn't wear her heart on her sleeve, but her puffed-up face, as if she had been crying a lot recently, and the ankle-length black dress under the sacking apron, as she paused there in her muddy gum-boots, with a bucket of feed in her red paw, told him that the worst had happened to her husband, Emil.

'Is it him?' he asked softly.

She didn't answer for a moment, but rubbed one hand against her plump cheek, the skin rasping under the rough surface of her palm; then she crooked a finger at him and stomped around the house to where they kept the pigs.

A heap of fresh earth was piled there, covered with meadow flowers, a rough wooden cross stuck in its centre. He hesitated and then looked at the name which she had obviously burnt on it with a red-hot poker. It was his, although she had spelled it with two 'l's.

'What happened?' he asked after a while . . .'Why did you bury him here like this?'

Madame Lejeune pushed away the Fleming foal which was nosing the pocket of her apron, obviously looking for some titbit she kept there. 'They killed him. The Walloons from over there in Old Belgium,' she pointed to the next ridge-line which had marked the border between Belgium and Germany prior to 1918. 'Beat him to death with clubs.'

'But in God's name, why, Madame?' Otto asked in horror.

'They said he was a German nationalist, whatever that may be, and wanted to return the East Cantons to the Prussians . . . And then in St Vith they wouldn't bury him in the cemetery because the director is one of those new Nazis and he said that Emil was pro-Belgian and not fit to lie at the side of good Germans.'

Otto shook his head sadly, suddenly aware for the first time in his young existence that life was really a tragedy and that in the end everything had to go bad, one way or another. 'What can I say, Madame?' he asked weakly.

'Nothing. Come, let me make you a good Ardennes bacon sandwich and a cup of real bean coffee, remember?'

He nodded.

'*Mon Dieu!*' she exclaimed, 'how my Emil did laugh every time he remembered the look on your face the first time you came here and we gave you the coffee for the Prussian shit!' She stomped towards the kitchen, chuckling and crying at the same time.

'Uniforms,' the Count had announced solemnly. 'To be exact, twelve uniforms are what we need.'

Otto had said nothing.

'We want six border guards' uniforms, two tram conductors, two street-gang overseers' uniforms like they wear over there in Belgium,' the Count had ticked them on his fingers, 'and two gendarme uniforms.'

Otto remained stubbornly silent.

The Count, dressed in an immaculate white dressing-gown, complete with monogram in gold on the pocket, had frowned and then continued. 'As soon as Father Christmas heard we had a Belgian expert, the assignment came winging its way here.'

'Expert?'

'Yes, of course, you,' the Count had said, his face serious. 'Everyone knows that you know that part of the world, like the back of your hand. That's why I picked you for training in the first place.' Otto had sighed. In the years to come he would learn that all the members of the *Abwehr*, and for all he knew, their opposite numbers in France and England, believed their own lies; it was one of their greatest faults.

'Where will you begin?' And then before Otto could explode, he had added, 'Old Father Christmas had indicated to Gertie that there will be five thousand reichsmark expenses in it, you know for travel, bribes etc, and a five-thousand-mark bonus on the successful delivery of the uniforms.'

Otto's mouth opened and closed abruptly like a drowning man gasping for breath before he went down for the third and last time. 'Five-thousand-mark bonus!' he had choked.

'That's what Old Father Christmas said. Now where will you start?'

Otto hadn't the faintest idea who old Father Christmas was but he was offering a small fortune and that knowledge made his mind race at a furious pace as he considered a means of getting his hands on to that fortune.

Outside the mad map-reading instructor was burning away the foundations of the house with a blow torch and through the opening window, Otto could hear him moan, '*My God, they're everywhere!*' 'Curious chap,' the Count had commented, following the direction of Otto's gaze. 'Never touches a drop of the stuff either. Must be those damn grid references.'

'I have a contact,' Otto had said hesitantly, 'in Belgium.'

'I say, have you?'

'Yes,' he had lied glibly, emboldened by the knowledge that everyone in the *Abwehr* was crazy. 'He has a large landhouse not far from the German border.' He thought of Emil's tumbledown farmhouse and hoped there was no such thing as mental telepathy. 'He's a very high-ranking official.'

'But can he be trusted? Old Father Christmas has said that there must be the strictest security for this operation.'

'He's virtually one of us.'

'Good, you know your Belgium and your Belgians,' the Count had conceded. 'I'll leave it up to you. Now what about your code-name?'

'Code-name?'

'Of course, can't have an op without a code-name. Old Father Christmas wouldn't like that one bit.' The Count's handsome brow had creased in thought; then he had clicked his fingers together excitedly. 'Got it. What about *lobo*?'

'Lobo?'

'Yes,' he had said eagerly. 'It's Spanish for wolf.'

'I don't feel like a wolf. Besides it seems a damn silly name to me. I mean who would go around calling himself "wolf", I ask you?' Otto had sneered.

'Damn silly name, you think?' the Count had said mildly. 'Hm, funny that. You know, the Fuhrer has used the code-name "wolf" for the last twenty-odd years.'

Outside the smoke from the burning foundations of the *Abwehr*'s training school started to rise in a thick black cloud. Otto gave up.

Now Madame Lejeune wiped the tears from her broad ruddy country face and gave him a toothless smile, obviously delighted to have a man in the house again and one who did justice to her humble food. Not wishing to disappoint her, Otto took another bit of the enormous doorstep she had prepared for him, politely averting his gaze from the cup of coffee.

'Something worrying you?' she asked. 'You haven't deserted from the Prussians, have you, Otto?'

He smiled again at her use of the word 'Prussian'. 'Not really Madame, I'm not even a soldier. But I have been sent over by our authorities to make some – er – purchases over here in Belgium.'

'Coffee . . . cigarettes?'

'No, not exactly . . .' He put down his sandwich. 'Uniforms to be exact.'

'Uniforms, that's strange. I always thought you Prussians had uniforms enough of your own.' She reached forward and with her forefinger spooned out yet another dead fly from Otto's cup. They kept falling from the flypaper suspended directly above the battered kitchen-table at which the two of them sat. The flypaper, a fading photograph of Emil and Madame on their wedding day, and a wooden crucifix were the poor little place's sole decorations. 'You can have poor Emil's for nothing,' she said. 'And his medals for bowling too, if you want, Otto. The Belgians wouldn't allow him to wear his Iron Cross the Prussians gave him in the First World War, so he always wore his bowling medals at official functions.'

Inwardly Otto groaned. What a country Belgium was! Aloud he said, 'That's very kind, Madame. I'll pay you for it, of course. But I need more. I mean where do you get official uniforms around here – St Vith?'

She shook her head firmly. 'Oh, no, those pigs of Walloons in Old Belgium like to keep their dirty paws on as much business as they can. No, we of the East Cantons have to buy our uniforms in Verviers from the Walloons.'

'They don't speak German down there?'

'No, just their own *welsch** . . . French,' she added hastily, when she saw that he didn't understand the local term.

'I see,' Otto said gloomily. His original plan had been simplicity itself. Give Emil the five thousand marks in expense money and let him organise the uniforms by

* Local term for any foreign tongue.

legitimate means, pocketing what was left over for himself. But that was impossible now.

Suddenly Otto's gaze fell on the dead Emil's revolver in its big black holster, hanging from a nail beside the crucifix. In their typically sloppy way, the Belgian authorities had obviously forgotten to come and collect it. As if by magic, the whole plan presented itself in his head. Dressed in Emil's uniform, he could walk into the shop in Verviers where they produced the uniforms, draw the revolver and demand the uniforms. Then his face dropped. He couldn't even speak enough French to say 'hands up', not to mention state his demands.

For a long time the two of them sat at the battered kitchen-table, listening to the wind in the big poplars outside the house and the soft crackle of the wood burning in the stove in a corner, while Otto worried on his problem, and Madame Lejeune occupied herself once more with her knitting.

'Madame, do you speak French . . . er . . . *welsch*?' Otto broke the heavy silence at last.

Madame Lejeune put down her knitting – it was for a male sock. Even though Emil was dead, she still knitted them for him out of habit. 'Yes, I speak the pigs' language. I worked in Verviers General Hospital as a scrub-maid for three years before I married Emil.'

'So,' Otto said thoughtfully, absorbing the information, telling himself that the new plan forming in his fertile mind was crazy, but that these days everything seemed crazy to him, and because of that it might just work. He licked his dry lips and wished that he had had a good glass of cold Berlin Kindl beer in front of him at this moment instead of the cup of fly-filled coffee. Gingerly he picked out a fly and left it to die on the table, kicking its legs valiantly to the very last, taking his time, wondering if the big-bosomed farm-woman opposite him wouldn't break out into mad laughter when he made his mad proposal; and then abruptly in one quick burst of words, he blurted it out, '*Madame Lejeune, would you like to earn five thousand marks?*'

THREE

At first everything went perfectly.

They arrived in Verviers, exactly as planned, just as the provincial town was beginning to wake up once more from its midday sleep, and the storekeepers were starting to take down the shutters which barred their doors once again. But the streets were relatively empty. The grey drizzle was keeping the locals indoors and reducing the number of cyclists. Those few pedestrians who were about walked slowly and with their heads bent deep into the upturned collars of their coats, as if weighed down by the weather and the times. They clattered along the cobbled road that led by the gaudy nineteenth century main station at a smart pace, she in her best black, with a sack around her shoulders to keep off the rain, and apparently composed; he dressed in Emil's uniform, with one of his shabby raincoats concealing the uniform, and definitely not composed, though he did not show his companion on the cart that. In his short criminal life after he had run away from Stralsund, Otto had committed quite a number of petty crimes, but he had never yet taken part in armed robbery, especially one which would take place in a foreign country.

Now the fleming's pace began to slacken as the cobbled road grew steeper beyond the *Gare* and they began to ascend to the upper half of the Walloon city in which lay the uniform store they had come to rob.

Minutes passed, while she guided him effortlessly through the maze of nineteenth century cobbled streets, heavy with the smell of the raw beef tartare, which the Walloons loved, and the stench of urine from the city's poorly functioning drainage system. In years to come Otto would have long forgotten the details of his first robbery, but he would always be able to recall that smell.

'There,' she whispered and pointed to a store to their right. Its windows were filled with old-fashioned legless and headless dummies, clad in a varied selection of official uniforms. At their feet lay waxed, moustached heads in military-style caps, which made them look as if they had just been beheaded. 'That's it.'

He nodded his understanding and urged the fleming further up the road, before doing a U-turn and then tying the horse's reins to a convenient lamp-post after pulling the brake. 'Easier this way,' he whispered.

She smiled at him with toothless gums, her eyes sparkling with excitement. 'I know,' she said eagerly. 'Downhill for a quick get-away, eh? Oh yes, me and Emil were great ones for the thrillers. Once a year regular we went to the cinema in St Vith to see the gangsters.' She closed one eye and swung an imaginary machine-gun from her fat hip, making clicking sounds.

'Oh, no!' Otto groaned, while she beamed at him.

'Come on.'

'This is going to be fun,' she said and let herself be escorted to the uniform store.

They had gone over the plan a dozen times. She, naturally, would do the talking, in this case, *reading*, for however much she tried, she could not memorise the list of uniforms and so in the end he had been forced to print them for her on a piece of paper. Once inside the store, she would read them to the, hopefully, patient storekeeper.

Of course, he would then demand her authority for collecting official uniforms. He would open his raincoat to reveal Emil's uniform, which hopefully would do the trick. If that didn't work, another thousand-franc note, placed on the top of the pile she would put on the counter to prove her good faith before she began reading off her list, should clinch matters. At least that was Madame Lejeune's opinion. As she had remarked contemptuously several times on the long drive to Verviers: 'Your average Walloon pig would sell his own mother for a five-franc piece.'

Otto hesitated only a fraction of a second at the entrance to the dingy little store, then he took his courage in both hands and opened the door to the clatter of the bell above them.

Almost instantly a small, bespectacled figure emerged from behind the thick felt curtain to the back of the place, tailor's measure around his neck, thread hanging out of the corner of his mouth, body stooped with years of bending over his sewing. '*Bonjour*,' he croaked.

'*Bonjour*,' they replied and Otto waited awkwardly, as Madame Lejeune started to pile the franc notes up in front of her on the dusty counter, while the little tailor stared at her, obviously bewildered.

With due ceremony, the farm-woman now drew out her list, tilting it slightly to the left to get the best of the light and after duly clearing her throat in the fashion of a child about to recite a poem for its teacher, she started to read off the list, while the tailor listened in silence, his bewilderment growing by the instant.

'*Pas possible*,' he croaked when she was finished and the manner in which he shook his head told Otto that it was his turn now. Feeling like some exhibitionist in one of Berlin's parks, he ripped open the shabby raincoat to reveal Emil's uniform below. '*Voilà!*' he said too loudly, using the word she had coached him to use.

The tailor was surprised, but not impressed. Again he shook his head and said, '*Pas possible! Sans autorisation, pas des uniforms. C'est la loi.*'

Madame Lejeune was unimpressed by his refusal. She held up a massive paw to stop the flow of words, as if she were a traffic cop at rush hour, and then when the tailor grew silent, she produced another one-thousand-franc note and laid it on the pile in front of her with a huge conspiratorial wink.

The tailor was impressed and Otto could see the conflicting emotions battling with each other inside him, but in the end his skinny yellow face hardened. Once more he shook his head firmly, scattering dandruff like snow onto his bent shoulders.

For what seemed an age, the three of them stood there in the dark shop: the big bluff woman, the handsome young policeman, and the hunchback. They might well have been characters at the end of the first act of some nineteenth century German farce, preparing the audience for the surprise, funny or otherwise, soon to come.

Abruptly it came from Madame Lejeune – and it wasn't funny, at least it wasn't for the hunchbacked tailor.

With surprising speed for such a big woman, she did two things. One hand grabbed at Otto's waist. Instinctively, in the fashion of all young men, he doubled up, hands covering his genitals. But it wasn't his eggs she was after, but his revolver. The other shot out and clutched the tailor's throat so hard that his yellow face went an abrupt purple and his eyes threatened to pop out of their sockets at any moment. '*Uniforms*,' she growled in best American gangster fashion, flourishing her husband's revolver beneath the terrified man's nose. '*Allez, vite . . . les uniforms, sale cochon!*'

'*Oui, oui*,' he hissed in a strangled voice, knees giving away beneath him with fear so that she was holding him there suspended in mid-air.

Talking out of the corner of her mouth, Madame Lejeune, her eyes gleaming with excitement – obviously enjoying every minute of this little drama – snapped, 'All right, Jo, Jo, take him inside. I'll cover the door.'

'*Jo, jo!*' Otto croaked helplessly, as Madame Lejeune

let go of the tailor. He staggered against the counter, eyes whirling wildly. Blindly he followed the trembling tailor to the back, where the latter started piling brand-new uniforms over Otto's outstretched arm, as if his very life depended upon it.

It was just as they were about to leave the scene of the crime that things started to go wrong. With the uniforms piled high across his outstretched arm, Otto waited impatiently, his other hand on the door handle, eager to be off, while Madame Lejeune, in complete charge of the situation, gave the ashen-faced little tailor her last instructions, emphasising her points with the big revolver. '*Cinq minutes, compris? . . . cinq minutes.*' She was ordering him to stay there, her broad face glowing with pleasure at this great adventure, better even than the films at St Vith's *Koenigliches Lichtspieltheater*, when the weapon exploded with a huge detonation.

Otto ducked hurriedly. Behind him the plate-glass window crumpled into a crazy gleaming spider's web of shattered glass. Slowly and dramatically, one of the dummies, sawdust pouring from a sudden hole in its stuffed chest, started to keel over. And then abruptly the little tailor was screaming, screaming, screaming, his eyes white, wild and wide with shock behind his glasses.

'Oh, Christ,' Otto gasped. 'Give me that damned shooting-iron!' He grabbed the big black revolver out of her suddenly nerveless fingers and then they were off, pelting for the cart, the fleming rearing up on his hind-legs, flailing the air with alarm, Otto's ears already taking in the shrilling of police whistles and the cries of alarm growing louder on all sides in the narrow stone chasms of the dingy apartment houses.

For nearly six months now even since it had become obvious in the early summer of 1939 that there was going to be another war, the Walloon citizens of Verviers had been living on their nerves.

Daily they awaited the invasion of their mighty neighbour only twenty kilometres to the East, complicated by the fact that there were some seventy thousand former German citizens right on their own doorstep in Belgium's eastern cantons. As if that weren't bad enough there were new and frightening rumours every second week that the local Flemings were going to rise against the ruling Walloons, supported by the perfidious English, just across the border in France, who were only too eager to incorporate the Province of Liège into the Empire upon which the sun never set.

It was not surprising, therefore, that the accidental shot fired in the little military tailor's shop set off an immediate panic in the provincial Walloon township. The rumours fled from street to street with the speed of light. '*A policeman had been shot up at the tailor's . . . a couple of dozen people had seen his dead body among the shattered glass . . . Somehow the Boche were involved because someone had heard the killers call out in German as they had escaped on horseback . . . They were using cavalry too . . . There was no denying that . . . Many citizens had seen or heard their horses galloping furiously from the scene of the murder . . .*'

'*THE UHLANS . . . THE UHLANS ARE HERE!*' that dreaded word went up everywhere; and even the little children, who had been born decades after the Uhlans had first cantered into Verviers in 1914 knew what that meant.

Franc-tireurs began firing from house windows everywhere. Refugees threw their most treasured possessions into the traditional dog-carts and started to flee the doomed city at once. Up on the heights on the road to Liège, a green, anti-aircraft crew, panicked by the news, narrowly missed shooting down the scheduled 14.00 hours Sabena flight from Cologne-Wahn to Brussels. Down in the old town, long-haired, excited youths started to loot the Jewish quarter. But that was nothing new. In Verviers they always looted the Jewish quarter in moments of panic and danger.

Madly Madame Lejeune lashed the sweating fleming as the swaying cart rattled through the crazy streets, while Otto hung on for dear life, the precious uniforms clutched to his chest, big revolver held tightly in his free hand, determined that she would not get her fingers on it again, muttering to himself in wide-eyed amazement, as he viewed the crazy scenes all around, 'But we only robbed a few uniforms . . . only a few uniforms!' In a wild kaleidoscope of screaming, crazy people, pistol shots, the flames of burning buildings, twisting, turning streets, they bolted for freedom the way they had come, down the hill into the lower town, past the nineteenth century station, where already the mob was fighting to escape by 'the last train', as the panic-stricken rumour had it (it was only going as far as the next goods station), into the maze of mean working-class streets that led out of the town.

As the minutes flew by, Otto's heart started to resume its normal beat. They were going to do it; they were going to make their escape without any further trouble. And then it happened. Like a slow locked dream.

A hundred metres further up the road, a black Citroen stopped and as the cart rattled towards it, three heavy-set men, with felt hats pulled down well over their foreheads, got out of it, their hands reaching into their inside pockets automatically. Otto did not need Madame Lejeune's excited '*Polizei!*' to tell him who they were. He would have recognised them as 'bulls' a kilometre away. What was he going to do?

'Get out of the way!' he cried in German. '*Get out!*'

The three men didn't move. Instead they planted themselves firmly in the path of the flying cart, pistols appearing in their hands as if by magic.

Otto fired instinctively, just as 'Gertie', the Commandant, had taught him to.

The first man's knees gave way suddenly beneath him. Abruptly a blood-red flower exploded dramatically at his chest. His face took on that expression, which Otto would get to know so well in the terrible years to come, one of surprise, even indignation as he realised he had been cheated of life. Next instant the Walloon slammed to the dirty cobbles and the cart was through, followed by stabs of scarlet flame, which grew wilder and more ineffective by the instant. One moment later they were careering around the corner on one crazy wheel, with the green hills of the Ardennes looming up in front of them at a tremendous rate. They had done it!

FOUR

'*Gratulière*,' the Count said impulsively, his plump affected face wreathed in smiles. 'I knew you'd do it. You have carried out your first assignment as we had expected you would. Just like the professional you are.' Otto let his hand be shaken, but said nothing, his face sombre and brooding.

For an instant the Count seemed to return to the world of the sane as he recognised the look. 'You killed a man, my boy, but it couldn't be helped. You can't make an omelette without cracking eggs. It was an act of war.'

'But we're not at shitting war with Belgium!' Otto blurted out hotly. '*Are we?*'

But the Count wouldn't be drawn, just as the uniformed *Abwehr* official from Berlin, who had taken the seemingly precious uniforms from him half an hour before and had disappeared heading east again at high speed, had revealed nothing. Instead he said, his voice its normal fruity self once more, 'It was a stroke of genius to disguise your accomplice as a woman. That really set the cat among the pigeons. According to our informants on the border, the whole eastern part of the country is in an uproar. They're stopping women on the streets everywhere and making them strip in public to prove their gender. There'll be questions asked in the Belgian Senate tomorrow morning, you mark my words, Otto.' He beamed at a morose Otto. 'By the way where is the chap now?'

'Oh, he's all right,' Otto replied reluctantly.

'Gone to ground no doubt!'

'Something like that,' Otto agreed, remembering Madame Lejeune's own phrase. 'I'm gonna take a dive, Otto,' she had said after he had given her the five thousand francs, using that pseudo-gangster slang borrowed from the pictures which she now affected. 'This cabbage will keep me nicely holed up in the hills with my sister beyond Eupen for a good while. The bulls'll never find me up there.' He shook his head with despair at the memory. It seemed everybody touched by this shitting spy business went slightly crazy, even the damnfool cop who had tried to stop him in that cobbled backstreet. Any person in his right mind would have simply jumped out of the way; he knew he would have done.

'I see,' the Count said, mistaking the sombre look on Otto's face for something else. 'You don't have to tell me any more. You're protecting your operatives, I know.' He nodded his silver-grey head in approval. 'I'd do the same.'

Otto dismissed a confident Madame Lejeune with her new slang and her new tough manner of talking out of the side of her mouth, and waited numbly for what was to come now.

'And now, Otto, I've got a very big surprise for you,' Count von der Weide said excitedly.

'Don't tell me the Fuhrer has turned out to be a male impersonator?' Otto said sourly.

The Count didn't seem to hear. 'Otto, my boy, this evening you will be given the great honour of meeting the head of our service. He wishes to give you your well-earned bonus personally, congratulate you, and discuss a little scheme with you.' There was an uneasy look in the Count's eyes which Otto nearly missed, but before Otto could remark upon it, the Count hurried on with, 'Tonight, Otto, you will meet old Father Christmas himself . . .'

Otto hardly recognised the spy-school mess. Everything had been painted fresh and bright seemingly overnight and there was only the faintest smell of burnt wood from the fire. The spy-school personnel must have worked like the devil to get the place presentable so quickly for the surprise visit of their mysterious chief. On all sides there were great vases of expensive flowers, the silver gleamed in the warm yellow light cast by the candelabra which ranged the length of the long festive table, and everywhere those of the staff who were officers were dressed in their gala uniforms complete with decorations, bowing and toasting and chatting animatedly with each other, as if it were weeks not hours since they had last seen one another.

Even old Hirsch, one of the civilians, had changed his usual grubby, baggy blue suit for what appeared to be some sort of Italian peasant costume, complete with large gold earrings under the flowered scarf wound round his head, whereas Maps seemed quite restrained and normal for this time of day, save for the fly-whisk he carried with which he occasionally swatted something, seen only by his crazed eye.

Otto accepted a drink from one of the white-coated mess waiters and idly watched Brass Eggs in his immaculate uniform talking animatedly with what looked like a North African, dressed in a funeral black suit and holding a pair of expensive-looking dachshunds, one of which had just made a puddle against the gleaming riding boot of Major Haase, though as yet the red-faced Commandant had not become aware of that particular fact.

Otto frowned. The man with the dachshunds was the only man in the room he did not know. Was he the mysterious Father Christmas? He looked important enough and Brass Eggs was laying on the soft-soap very thick, as if the unsmiling North African might be the one. But would Germany's world-wide spy organisation be run by a foreigner? Otto asked himself. He shrugged. In the *Abwehr* anything was possible.

'You, *Tedesci*, really have a sense of occasion, *caro* Otto,' Hirsch, who had been born not more than five hundred metres from where Otto had been in Berlin, said at his side in a thick Italian accent. He thrust out his hand at the glittering table. '*Molto bene!*' he breathed in admiration. 'Unfortunately, we Italians lack your German talent for *organizatione*.' He shook his head and his gold earrings rattled noisely. 'But our beloved *Duce* is trying, Otto. One day he will make us as the Romans of old.' His hand shot out and he clicked to attention. '*Eviva il Duce!*'

Presuming that some toast had been given, officers everywhere snapped to attention and raised their glasses in salute. The air was full of *Heil Hitler* and 'Long live Italy'.

Otto downed his drink in one go and seized another one from a passing waiter; he needed it this night.

Five minutes later the room was alerted to the fact that dinner was about to be served by the soft sound of a gong being struck in the anteroom. All conversation ceased immediately and every gaze concentrated on the little group poised at the entrance to the mess.

The Count was in front, resplendent in what appeared to be a white silk hussars' uniform, complete with slung cloak, edged with fur, *sabretache* and dangling sabre, though for the life of him Otto couldn't identify the uniform's origin. Perhaps the Count had created it for himself; he wouldn't put it past him. Behind the Count there was a little man, dressed in a white apron and tall cook's hat, ready to push the dumb-waiter into the room upon which rested a great silver salver from which the hot steam curled. He was flanked by two kitchen assistants, who towered above the diminutive, middle-aged cook, both armed with great carving knives. The Count nodded and with himself in the lead, moving forward ceremoniously by means of a strange little mincing step, half-dance, half-walk, the little procession filed to the table along the line of officers who clapped politely with white-gloved hands.

Next to Otto, Hirsch carried away, presumably, by his Latin temperament, cried exuberantly, '*Eviva . . . eviva!*'

The little cook smiled at the excited Jew and assuming that he was speaking Spanish, called out the menu to Hirsch in that language, '*Pastel de patatas con aceitunas negras, con habas a la catalana y pollo relleno ingles.*'

Hirsch looked puzzled, then whispered finally to Otto, 'I don't like that rich French food. Plays havoc with my stomach.'

Otto laughed softly. 'It smells good at least,' he said and followed the Count's order to be seated. Immediately there was a burst of excited chatter as the lids covering the silver dishes were lifted and the officers were able to see their contents, while standing next to the dumb-waiter the middle-aged cook flushed with undisguised pleasure.

Swiftly the two assistants got to work carving the stuffed chicken and heaping on the creamed potatoes, decorated with black olives, ladling out portions of steaming beans, resplendent with much garlic, then handing each gold-rimmed plate to the red-faced, hot cook, who hurried down the table to place it in front of the guests with an extravagant flourish.

Finally each guest had been served and was staring down at his steaming heaped plate in hungry anticipation, save Maps who was turning over his chicken gingerly, as if he half expected to find a little green man hidden beneath it, while the cook beamed at them, obviously happy that the prospect of eating his food gave the assembled company such pleasure.

The Count rose to his feet at the bottom of the table. '*Herr Admiral, darf ich bitten?*' he requested very formally. Otto followed the direction of his gaze, puzzled. He seemed to be talking to the cook!

The cook smiled. With due ceremony, he removed his cook's tall hat and handed it to the man with the dogs who had appeared, as if in response to some signal, and who had taken up his position behind the cook. A was whipped off to reveal the dark blue uniform, heavy with gold braid on the sleeve, of a full admiral in the *Kriegsmarine.** Adjusting his tie slightly, the Admiral strode to the head of the table and took his place there, bowing his snow-white head that gave him the look of a benign Father Christmas in spite of his dark, mysterious eyes.

Otto took a frantic swig at his *moselle*. He didn't need to be told who the man now sitting at the head of the table, making animated conversation with his high-ranking neighbours was. He was 'Father Christmas', the head of the Third Reich's world-wide espionage system, and he had just cooked Otto's dinner!

'Monsieur Stahl,' Admiral Canaris, old Father Christmas, said solemnly, while outside the drunken singing that was dying away in the distance indicated that the party was finally over, 'in Berlin the Fuhrer has made an irrevocable decision.'

Otto said nothing. He couldn't; he was still too bemused by the events of that evening. Even the fact that the little spy-master seemed to take him for a Belgian, (although there was no mistaking his, Otto's, Berlin accent) did not move him.

The Admiral nodded to his North African servant. 'Mohamed, take the dogs out now.'

'As my master wishes,' the body-servant said and gave a low, ceremonial bow, touching his dusky hand to his forehead before leaving with the suddenly excited, yelping dogs.

At the door, Brass Eggs, his face flushed with drink and his collar ripped open, said, 'I'll look after him, sir.'

'Thank you, you are very kind,' Canaris said.

Brass Eggs thrust his arm eagerly through the North African's and they went out, rather too hurriedly, Otto couldn't help thinking.

* The German Navy.

The Admiral waited till the door had closed behind them before turning to Otto and the Count once more. 'It is an unfortunate decision for your brave little country, Monsieur Stahl,' he said, 'at least at first. Perhaps later on it will prove a blessing in disguise. *Am deutschen Wesen soll die Welt genesen*,'* he quoted the old Imperial saying, with a smile on his thick lips, though those dark hooded eyes of his did not light up.

'Yessir,' Otto said woodenly.

From outside there came little excited gasps of delight and once a small, quickly suppressed moan of pain. Idly Otto wondered just exactly how Brass Eggs and Mohamed were exercising the Admiral's sausage-dogs.

'Stahl,' the Admiral continued, 'the Fuhrer has decided that it is necessary that German forces invade and occupy your Fatherland in order that we can outflank the Maginot Line. It is unfortunately the only way that we can overcome that obstacle and defeat our Anglo-French enemies.'

'I see, sir.'

The little Admiral nodded his approval. 'You are taking the news well, Stahl,' he said. 'But it is only what I expected from an agent of your calibre . . . Now, we of the *Abwehr* have an important part to play in this new operation. Not only will our brave Brandenburgers take part in the initial frontier attacks, but some of us have a significant role in the preparations for those attacks.'

He looked firmly at Otto and with a sinking feeling Otto half-guessed that the little Admiral was referring specifically to him.

'Monsieur Stahl, after that recent coup which you pulled off so spectacularly, who is better fitted for the new task ahead?' He lowered his voice to a whisper. 'The Our bridges,' he hissed, as if the words were of great significance and touched the side of his nose conspiratorially.

* Roughly, 'the world will thrive through Germany'.

Otto suppressed a moan with the greatest of difficulty. Five minutes later, accompanied by a beaming Mohamed and Brass Eggs who looked slightly worse for wear, the little Admiral left. But before he did so, he paused at the door and whispered something to the Count.

Otto was not particularly interested – he was too preoccupied with whatever new misery old Father Christmas had dreamed up for him – but he did catch the words, 'Fuhrer . . . Munster-Eifel . . . some time in April . . .' before the Admiral disappeared with the yapping dogs at his heels. Then the words meant nothing to him, but later, much later, they would become significant, very significant indeed.

'Tomorrow morning at zero eight hundred hours,' the Count's voice broke into his gloomy reverie.

Otto looked up. Meadow was very pale, as if he had just received a sudden shock. Otto wondered why.

FIVE

'The bridges across the River Our, here at Losheim,' the Count pointed to the map spread between them on the table, 'and here at Andler. Not very large, as you can see, but if the Belgians were to destroy them, the river would present a serious obstacle for our armoured thrust around the flank of the Maginot Line through the Belgian Ardennes.'

'I'm not going,' Otto said sourly.

Count von der Weide seemingly didn't hear. 'Naturally we know about them in a general way. They are not exactly new. But we don't know the strength of the garrisons presently manning them, the nature of their defensive positions and the exact location of the explosive chambers in the bridges themselves. All vital information, of course.' He paused and looked at Otto in his usual winning manner.

'Now look here, Meadow,' Otto said angrily. 'I've had enough of this damnfool game! Don't you realise that they'll be looking for me over there? I've killed a bloke – I'm a wanted man!'

'That shouldn't worry an agent of your calibre,' he said maddeningly. 'You've probably done things like that a dozen times or more in the past. Ice-water runs through that chap's veins, those were the very words the Admiral used to me last night about you. *Nomen est—*'

'Now don't start that damn carry-on again!' Otto exploded, his temper rising by the instant. 'You know as plain as that big nose on your damn face, that I am an ordinary working-class lad from Berlin who, up to two months ago, was driving a shit-wagon at the *Westwall*. I'm no super-agent and have no desire to become one. I'll put my cards on the table, Meadow. I left Berlin last August to find a nice cushy safe billet where I could sit out this war without getting my stupid turnip blown off by some stupid Polack, Frog or Tommy. Do you get it, Count – S-A-F-E?' He spelled out the word furiously, his face red with anger. His shoulders heaving a little with the effort of talking so much, he ended weakly with, 'Count, in truth, I am a devout coward.'

'Oh, I can hardly believe that, Otto,' the Count said mildly. 'But calm yourself, my dear young friend. Listen to my offer first.'

'Offer?'

'Yes, offer. Get me the information I require and I'll ensure you have your safe billet for the rest of this war.'

Otto eyed him suspiciously. 'Where?' he demanded.

'Here.'

'What – at the spy-school?'

'Yes, Otto. As an instructor. You see we have urgent need of an experienced instructor in our clandestine-operations section. I mean none of the staff have had actual field experience. In essence they are all theorists.'

'That you can say again,' Otto said sourly and considered the proposition. At the spy-school, they were all nuts, of course, but they were safe nuts.

'The Our bridges are just over the Belgian frontier. It would be a matter of a day's work and you would be perfectly safe,' the Count urged, obviously realising that Otto was thinking the matter over.

'What would the pay be?'

'As a civilian instructor?'

'Yes, *civvie*,' Otto said hastily. 'There's going to be no military uniform for Mrs Stahl's son, thank you very kindly.'

The Count pursed his lips. 'Three to four hundred

marks a month, expenses naturally—'

'Naturally.'

'And free board. Only officers pay the mess-bills. Otto it would be the equivalent to the salary of a leading employee in a big city office.'

Otto bit his bottom lip. The pay was very good. It would be twice the best wage he had ever earned in Berlin, and the Count was right: the spy-school was definitely a cushy and very safe billet. No one in his right mind would ever send its instructors to battle; they would lose the war for Germany before the day was out. 'All right,' he said grudgingly, 'I'll do it. Just once more . . . But Meadow, how am I to set about it? I know nothing about military matters. For example, how do I find out the number of the garrison? I mean, I can hardly ask them to stand up and kindly be counted?'

The Count beamed, happy that Otto had decided to go ahead with the assignment. 'Not necessary, old chap. It can be done more obliquely than that. By loaves.'

'By loaves?'

'Yes. Count the daily ration of loaves delivered to the garrison, divide the number by the Belgian Army's official daily bread ration, taking into account that NCOs and officers get a slightly larger allowance, and you've got your number.'

Otto controlled his exasperation with difficulty. 'And how am I to know how much bread a Belgian soldier gets daily?' he asked, his voice heavy with sarcasm.

The Count did not notice it. 'Not to worry, Otto,' he answered easily. 'We've got clever books with all that sort of thing in them, at least we should have.'

'All right.' Otto gave in on that point. 'What about their positions? How am I going to discover them?'

Again the Count had his answer ready. 'Mushrooms . . . you'll be collecting mushrooms.'

'What!'

'Yes. Nobody ever notices a chap collecting mushrooms, it's such a nice peaceful pursuit, and it blends in with the countryside. I mean everyone expects to see moment later he followed this with the apron, which people collecting mushrooms when they're in the country.'

'But what if there *aren't* any mushrooms?' Otto objected, restraining himself with an effort of willpower.

The Count did not seem to hear. 'You circle their positions,' he said, his right arm moving back and forth picking imaginary mushrooms, 'apparently concentrating on the task in hand. Two mushrooms to the right of your basket indicate a machine-gun pit, three on the left side for a gun emplacement . . .'

Otto gave up. 'Count,' he said through gritted teeth, desperately trying to stop that flow of words, 'thanks for the tips. But I think I'd better do it my way.'

'Oh, all right, as you wish, Otto. You'd better see Hirsch about your false identity papers etc.' He thrust out his soft, well-manicured hand. 'I won't be seeing you before you go, Otto. I'm off on business to . . . er . . . Munster-Eifel.' For some reason, the Count lowered his gaze for an instant, as if he were embarrassed. 'So I'd like to wish you happy landings, now, Otto. I'm quite sure that you'll be completely successful.' The Count's smile was genuine.

'Thanks, Meadow,' Otto said, and then, as an afterthought, 'If there are any mushrooms, I'll bring you a basketful.'

SIX

'In the old days,' the sergeant said dourly, as they plodded through the ruined, shell-shattered Lorraine village, its cobbled streets littered with the debris of war, 'before folks like you and me got educated, they'd let yer average hairy-assed, old stubble-hopper enjoy hissen when he captured a place like this. You know, there'd be a high old time, raping the local gash and looting the sauce from the cellars. Licentious soldiery and all that. But not these days.' He aimed a vicious kick at the dead cat which lay in his path and it sailed through the air like a hairy football to disappear through the shattered window of the French cottage opposite.

'Goal!' Otto said.

His guide, the gloomy sergeant, did not seem to hear. 'No, these days, it's all talk of liberation and freedom and fighting for national survival and all that sort of crap,' he moaned. 'So we haven't *conquered* this goddam cow-town, we've *liberated* it.'

'I think I'd rather be conquered,' Otto observed. 'There isn't a roof left in the place.'

'Doesn't worry me much,' the sergeant said, staring at the naked beams with a professional eye, 'I'm a slater by trade in civvie street. They can blast the roof off'n every house from here to Frankfurt, I wouldn't mind. It'd keep me in fried taties and *bratwurst* for the rest of my days.'

'I expect it would,' Otto said, thinking that the dour

sergeant was the first sane person he had met in many a month. Then he remembered that in a few moments he would be entering enemy territory and that this was no time for philosophising on the sanity of the average man-in-the-street. 'What's the drill now, Sergeant?' he asked a little anxiously.

The NCO looked at him. 'You're starting to talk like an officer already,' he commented without rancour. 'Drill?' He sniffed. 'Up that lane there, bearing north towards them hills. That's the Lux frontier. But be careful, the Frogs are somewhere in position to yer right on that tree-line, though if they're smart this day, they'll be tucked up nice and warm in their holes, drinking that red wine of theirs and toasting their sweaty frog feet.' He shivered dramatically. 'It's getting right back-end. I wouldn't be a bit surprised if we didn't have snow soon.' He stuck out his hand, without taking the glove off. 'All right, mate, this is as far as I go. Keep yer nose clean. I won't take my glove off cos I'm not an officer and gent, see.'

'Yes, I see.' Suddenly Otto felt quite scared. He would have dearly loved to have asked the NCO to stay with him a little longer, but he knew that couldn't be. The man was impatient to be off back to their own lines and the warm underground bunker from which he had been detailed by his officer to escort this strange-looking civilian with his onions and ancient rusting Frog cycle through no-man's land.

'And if yer get any of that Frog gash,' the sergeant said, his face cracking into a mean smile, 'don't wash your salami. Bring it back and let me have a smell. I'll dream of it when I'm kipping down with the five-fingered widow. Bye.'

'I'll do that. Bye.'

For a long time, Otto stood there in the wet dreary field watching the sergeant stride back down the cobbled road as if he were in a great hurry, feeling very exposed and very lonely; then when the NCO had disappeared around the corner, he remembered where he was and the danger he might well be in. Even at this moment some hidden Frenchman might be observing him through his field-glasses. Hastily, he swung round his bike, the handlebars laden with strings of onions that were already beginning to stink, and started to push down the track which led to Luxemburg.

It had been Hirsch's suggestion to have Otto slip through the tiny piece of French Lorraine held by the *Wehrmacht* as the result of a successful local offensive in late October, just after the end of the Polish campaign. 'But it seems a very long way round, Number Nine,' he had protested, using Hirsch's old code-name because he had forgotten the new one. 'Maybe to you, Sunray,' Hirsch had said, pointedly using Otto's new code-name. 'But Lorraine is the backdoor and undangerous. From there you can make your way into Luxemburg and then cross the frontier into Belgium. It's unguarded because they have had a customs union these many years. Much easier that way than going in through the front door. You can take it from me,' he said with a knowing look, as if he knew the Belgian frontier like the back of his grubby hand, 'that Belgium's border with the Reich is exceedingly well guarded.'

'I suppose you're right,' Otto had conceded.

'I know I am right,' Hirsch had snapped and, assuming that Otto's wan look indicated fear, he had pressed his arm firmly and said, '*coraggio, caro Otto*. Remember, we must be as the Romans of old.' He had clicked to attention and given Otto the fascist salute and that had been that. Now as Otto toiled up the narrow track towards Luxemburg, with a journey of nearly a hundred kilometres in front of him, he wondered a little uneasily whether Octavio (the little Jew had recently bestowed upon himself the imperial-sounding Roman name instead of the 'Izzy' that had been his for fifty-odd years) Hirsch had not been mistaken.

Still it was too late now to change the plan, he told

himself, and pushed hard at the damn bike. Pierre Kirschmeyer, Luxemburg onion-seller, he was and would remain until his mission was completed.

The road north through Luxemburg City, Diekirch, Ettelbruck and a series of mean villages, which looked as if they might well have been abandoned years ago, seemed one long uphill slog that got steeper and steeper by the kilometre. On the first morning of his journey through the little principality whose motto was 'we want to be left alone' (a sentiment with which a weary, sweating Otto heartily agreed), he tossed his stinking onions into the ditch. 'Excellent cover,' Hirsch had insisted. 'Onion-sellers are always wandering all over the place. Besides you can make a very good secret ink out of their juice at a pinch.' 'But who should I write to?' Otto had countered, but Hirsch had not been listening. That same afternoon the rusty French monster followed. The bike had been throwing its chain every kilometre or so and besides the hills of the *Luxemburgische Schweiz**, as the area was known by the locals, were too steep to ride up. He said goodbye to the bike without regret, marching on doggedly, an onion-seller without onions, his feet burning like fire.

By the evening of the first day, somewhere in the lonely hillside beyond the beer-brewing town of Diekirch, he was beat; and when it started to rain, a thin bitter grey drizzle as cold as a rich widow's heart, he decided he'd had enough. He had to find a place to get his head down for the night.

But there was not a house to be seen in that dreary empty rolling countryside, and perhaps because the drizzle made him keep his gaze lowered, he did not see the smoke curling out of a hole in the roof of the abandoned barn, to which he now headed as the only shelter seemingly available, until it was too late. The wizened,

* The Luxemburg Switzerland.

little toothless tramp in his ragged clothes sitting on a bundle of straw, roasting stolen potatoes on the prongs of a manure-fork smiled up at him and made a gesture that he should take a seat near the smoking fire with the words, 'lousy weather for tramps – and spies, isn't it?'

Roughly at that moment while Otto was attempting to recover from the shock of that greeting, Count von der Weide crouched in a large abandoned drainage pipe to shelter from the grey drizzle and surveyed the darkening wet countryside to his immediate front.

To the left there was the main road that led to Bad-Munster-Eifel, the walled medieval resort town of the area, while to the right there was the winding secondary road that ran through the sleepy little, slated-roofed village of Rodert and into the thick fir woods beyond.

Immediately to his front, however, lay the low camouflaged concrete shape of the 'Mountain-Nest', as it was code-named, surrounded by the protective guard-posts, 'Dora', 'Emil', 'Fritz', 'Arthur', 'Bruno' and naturally 'Caesar'. There had always to be something imperial about the places the Fuhrer chose for his secret headquarters.

He eyed the place, mentally penetrating the thick concrete walls, pinpointing the room occupied by Linge, the Fuhrer's body-servant, with next to it the bedroom of the Leader himself. If he was right in his assumptions, the Fuhrer would take his daily exercise, the walk with his alsation bitch, Blondi, just to the right of the bunker among the sparse young trees which had been planted to give the place additional camouflage. He closed one eye and squinted at the spot. The trees would present little problem, he told himself, even at this distance, which was over eight hundred metres, the closest he would be able to get without running the risk of alerting 'Post Caesar', immediately to his front.

Suddenly the Count started. There was the sound of slow footsteps like that of a bored man consigned to some wearisome, uninteresting task. He froze. A pair of highly polished black boots had halted in front of the pipe-end. He hardly dared breathe. Had he been discovered? Suddenly the unseen guard broke wind. The boots turned, spread apart. Count von der Weide wondered what was coming. Then there was the hiss of hot urine escaping from a sorely tried bladder. A frothing stream of dark yellow liquid started to pour into the pipe.

The Count tried to turn his head and escape it. To no avail. The confines of the pipe were too tight. Numbly, his eyes closed, he accepted his fate, the liquid trickling down his bent head, along his tightly clenched nostrils and dripping off his chin. Finally his ordeal was over and the SS guard started to stamp away, growing ever smaller in the circle of grey light at the end of the pipe.

'Geld verloren, nichts verloren
Ehre verloren, viel verloren
*Mut verloren, alles verloren**

The soaked Count whispered to himself, as he watched him go. Then he squeezed up one eye again and sighted along the length of the pipe, as if he were holding a rifle. '*Click*,' he snapped.

At that moment the black-uniformed, helmeted guard slipped in the mud of the forest trail and sat down suddenly in the goo, undoubtedly cursing as he did so.

Suddenly the Count smiled to himself. It seemed to be a good omen, he couldn't help thinking. Five minutes later he had gone, leaving the empty 'Mountain-nest' to disappear behind him into the grey drizzle.

* Roughly: 'Money lost, nothing lost. Honour lost, a lot lost. Courage lost, everything lost.'

SEVEN

'Ami, I'm called,' the toothless little tramp said, stretching out a dirty hand and breaking the heavy silence.

'Kirschmeyer,' Otto said thickly, remembering his new name at the very last moment. 'I'm a Luxemburg onion-seller.' The tramp winked at him and pulled down the corner of his right eye. 'See any green in there, comrade, eh?' he quipped, obviously not believing Otto's story one bit. 'Here,' he pulled one of the blackened potatoes off the end of the manure-fork and handed it to Otto, who yelped with pain.

'Shit,' he cursed, 'it's red hot.'

'There's salt in that tin there, if you want it,' the tramp said unfeelingly. 'I'm a child of the frontier,' he continued apropos of nothing. 'Grandmother a French whore to the Metz garrison, Grandfather a recruit in the Prussian Foot-Artillery, Year '88 and a chimney-sweep in civvy street, that goes without saying.' He winked at Otto knowingly. 'He poked Grandma well enough, all right. My old mother was the result, and of course, she followed in the family tradition. In 1918 when the Americans marched into Metz after the Battle of the Argonne, she was there waiting for them at the *Porte des Allemands*, with open arms – and other things, too, if you get my meaning.'

Otto spluttered through the burning-hot mouthful of potato that he got the general idea.

'Pregnant by the end of the week and I am the result, a

child of the frontier, as usual in this area, father unknown. So I call myself "Ami". . . short for "American", you know?'

Otto nodded he did.

For a while the little tramp ate in silence, as did Otto, while the wind howled outside and the rain lashed against the dirty cracked panes of the abandoned barn; but Otto kept stealing secret glances at his wrinkled, bronzed face, asking himself whether he had really heard those first cheerful words, 'Lousy weather for tramps – and spies.' Had the little tramp really said them?

But he had, for when Ami was finally finished with his stolen baked potatoes and had begun filling his little shag-pipe with tobacco, his casual question about who Otto was working for – the French or the Germans – indicated that his hearing had not been at fault thirty minutes before.

'What do you mean, working for them?' he asked, feigning indignation.

'Come off it, comrade,' Ami said easily, taking a deep contented draw at his pipe. 'All of us gents-of-the-road around here sell odd bits and pieces of information to both sides of the frontier. There's many a good chicken dinner and litre of wine I've had on the strength of the Maginot Line and the Westwall too. In winter it's that sort of thing that keeps yer average gent-of-the-road out of the shitting workhouse with all those damned white swans' (he meant nuns) 'with their bobbing and scraping and saying yer prayers and ringing shitting bells all the time.' He sniffed indignantly. 'It ain't godly some of the things those white swans want yer to do for a plate of pea soup and a bit of sour black bread.'

Otto was forced to smile at the little tramp's indignation. 'Do you mean to say then, that you're a . . .' he hesitated a fraction of a second over the word '. . . a spy?'

'Natch. I mean I'm no Mata Hari or anything like that. But it's a living, but you should know, comrade, You're in the same game yersen, aren't you?'

Otto did not answer and the little man shrugged good-humouredly. 'Have it your own way, comrade. But I'll tell you this.' He waited, and Otto was forced in the end to ask, 'What?'

'All this last week, comrade, I've been as sharp as a cut-throat razor. A couple of times I've even thought of doing harm to one of those sheep out there.' He licked his cracked lips. 'For the price of a jump with the girls in that fancy Catholic *puff* they've got up there in St Vith, I'll find out anything you want to know about this frontier.'

He looked hard at Otto, and the latter heard himself saying, 'I'll sleep on it.'

They crossed over the Luxemburg-Belgian border in grand style, in the back of the taxi which Ami had called to fetch them from the border village of Burg-Reuland, with the little tramp holding the back of the driver's seat rigidly and glass-eyed, as if willing the driver to get them to the *puff* more quickly. For his part Otto slumped in the upholstery, eyes closed, resigned to the fact that all his future life might well be like this: a crazy race through the night in foreign places, conducted against his will by fools and idiots, heading for the inevitable purposelessness, signifying nothing, profligate, wasteful, meaningless. It wasn't a pleasant thought.

The bolt was drawn finally after they seemed to have hammered at the door of the 'Catholic puff', as Ami called it, for a couple of years and the Madame stood there sternly. She was dressed in a gown of sequins that made her look like a fat mermaid with scales right up to her raddled neck.

'Money?' she demanded in a voice like that of a sergeant-major.

'Show her ladyship,' Ami said through toothless gums. 'Quick. I'm limping hard already!'

Otto opened his wallet and let her look inside with her beak-eyed gaze.

'*Bon*,' she said, 'thought you might be trying to palm some of those worthless marks off'n me. Wouldn't wipe my arse with those. Numbers five and three are free.' She glared at the little tramp. 'And remember, Ami, I know your dirty little tricks. None of yer titty-rolls, for a start. My girls are good nice clean persons. I don't want them to be spoilt.

'Of course, Madame,' Ami answered politely. 'But do you think one of your young virgins might see her way to holding it for me for a couple of seconds? I would be greatly indebted to her, if she would.'

The Madame fixed him with her hard gaze. 'One more word and I'll close the door in your face, Ami.'

The threat worked. Ami extended his hands, wrists together, as if he were waiting to have handcuffs clapped upon them. 'I'll come quietly, officer,' he said.

They passed in and before they parted to go their separate ways to the girls' cubicles, he whispered, 'Never fear, comrade, you'll get your information tomorrow.'

'I'd better,' Otto said, his face threatening.

Ami was unimpressed. 'I'll keep my boots on, then you'll be able to recognise me and pull me out of it,' were his last words and then he was tripping up the steps to Cubicle Five like an eager teenager going to get it for the first time.

They threw Ami out of the St Vith *puff* in the middle of the night. The bouncers' methods were not very gentle and decidedly not Christian. Without much ado, they heaved him out of the first floor window. In St Vith the bones of the burly farmboys who frequented the place did not break easily, but the racket Ami made breaking through the plate-glass awning of the bookshop in the first floor awoke Otto well enough. Seizing his clothes, knowing instinctively that it was his new acquaintance who had caused the racket, Otto hurried outside to find Ami alternately cursing and picking glass splinters from his skinny naked rump, while he searched around in the darkness for his clothes which the bouncers had thrown after him.

'What in three devils' name happened?' he demanded, hurrying into his own clothes.

'Not much,' Ami said with a yelp of pain. 'That was the trouble. Shitting high-class, hygienic Catholic *puff*! I just felt horny again, with the old love-juice right up to here, and she sez, as if it's important, "yer can't because it's past midnight. Now go back to sleep." And I sez to her, "What d'yer want – shitting double-time?" And she sez, I should mind my language, cos she was a decent girl. And I sez she shouldn't talk so much because I had ways of making her shut up, and I tried and she started screaming perversion and one thing led to another and—'

'They gave yer the old heave-ho?' Otto said without sympathy. 'Come on, get yer duds on. It's shitting freezing out here!'

Grumbling moodily to himself, the little tramp succeeded in finding the rest of his pathetic, ragged clothes, while Otto waited impatiently, stamping his feet in the freezing night air.

In silence they set off again, heading north towards the new dawn and the Our bridges, leaving a sleeping St Vith down below in the valley, but not before Ami had turned and shaken his little fist at the Belgian town, crying, 'Just you wait, you hygienic Catholic whores! One of these days I'll come back – and burn all yer Catholic candles! Then you'll be in a right old pickle.' And with that terrible threat uttered, he turned and stumped on in gloomy silence.

'*Merde!*' Ami said, as they stood at the end of the little gravelled country road and stared at the concrete bridge crossing the River Our at Andler, 'I could spit across that without even trying. Don't seem very important to me.'

Otto was forced to agree. The river couldn't have been more than ten metres' wide. Still the planners of the *Wehrmacht* thought it important enough. 'What now?' he asked, savouring the first warm rays of the winter sun, which filtered through the tall pines.

'Leave it to me,' Ami said confidently. 'These Belgies are used to us gents-of-the-road. Just you keep out of sight up there among the trees. I'll be back in a brace of shakes.' And with that, he was off, trudging down the road at a suitably slow pace for a tramp, whistling as if he hadn't a care in the world, this cold winter's morning.

Ten tense minutes passed leadenly and a worried Otto, hidden in the trees above the little road, was just telling himself once again that he hadn't the right kind of nerve for this spy business, when Ami came out of the little wooden hut to the right of the river bridge, munching a huge sandwich cheerfully waving to someone unseen inside.

Five minutes later he was up in the firs, hastily swallowing the rest of his bacon-sandwich and gasping, 'Paper and pencil! Quick! Before I forget!'

Laboriously, with his head twisted to one side and his face screwed up, obviously not used to writing, the little tramp put down the details Otto needed on the scrap of paper. 'A sergeant and twenty flat-footed soldiers,' he explained, pencilling in the number. He drew a shaky line for the bridge and circles to left and right of it. 'They've got a machine-gun post here and another one – here.' He marked a cross to the left-centre of the line which represented the bridge. 'That's where they've got the explosive chamber, but whether it's full of TNT or not, I couldn't tell yer.' He gave Otto the paper back with a grin of toothless triumph. 'Not bad, eh, even if I do say so myself.'

'But how did you do it?' Otto demanded. 'You weren't within fifty metres of the bridge. You were in the hut all the time. I know because I watched you.'

'Of course. But you know flat-footed soldiers? They've got no brains and they allus like to have things nice and tidy on charts and diagrams so that they can impress their generals when they come to inspect. I suppose it justifies all the money the tax-payers waste on the Army, like. So while I kept them busy, I ran my glassy orbits around the hut to see what they could see. Looki-looki, you know.'

'But how did you keep them busy, you little fart?' Otto demanded, 'and get a free sandwich as well?'

'With these.'

Like a magician producing one of his little surprises to his admiring audience, he pulled six or seven much-worn photographs out of his ragged sleeve.

Otto gasped.

They were pictures of two portly, middle-aged matrons with Eton crops, naked save for high-heeled shoes, performing several seemingly impossible acts together with the aid of what looked like a large policeman's rubber truncheon, their faces set and concentrated, as if it were a very serious business indeed and demanded full concentration. 'Dirty pictures!' Otto exclaimed.

'That's right,' Ami said easily, shoving them back up his sleeve once more. 'Nothing yer average flat-footed soldier likes better than a good dirty picture. Takes their minds off the monotony of their existence, I shouldn't wonder.' He sniffed. 'Gives them something worth dying for. Cunt's better than Fatherland any day!' He wiped his hand across his lips. 'Come on, comrade, let's be off to Losheim. With a bit of luck, I'll be there before they dish out the midday soup, and I'll say one thing for these Belgian Catholics, in spite of that business back there at St Vith, they *do* turn out a good drop of pea soup.' He raised his tiny little right leg and farted melodiously, as if in anticipation of the peas to come.

But obtaining the information they required at Losheim bridge turned out to be more difficult than at Andler. As before, the little tramp repeated the same performance, the casual walk to the guard hut, a few words with the sentry outside it and then, while Otto watched from his new hiding-place, he disappeared inside presumably to display his dirty pictures once more. Less tense now, Otto waited, noting that after Ami had been inside five minutes, a dour-looking man in the black uniform of the border-police, rifle slung over his big shoulder, entered.

Another few minutes passed. Suddenly and startlingly, things began to go wrong. The door of the hut flew open. Even at that distance, Otto could hear the exchange of heated, angry words, followed a moment later by Ami flying through the open door, propelled by the border-guard's big gleaming boot.

As he crouched there, momentarily dazed, the border-guard, crimson with anger, bellowed at the little tramp, unslinging his rifle as he did so, while behind the enraged guard, laughing soldiers looked at each other and pointed their fingers to their temples, as if to indicate to Ami that they knew the man was completely mad.

The laughter seemed to enrage the policeman even more. He levelled his rifle at Ami and bellowed some kind of order at him in Flemish.

'*Lat op*,' Otto could just make out Ami's reply. Presumably the words meant the border-guard should stop whatever he was about to do.

But the enraged man was too far gone to be stopped now. Again he bellowed an order at the little tramp, whose confident look had vanished now, jerking his rifle forward threateningly.

Instinctively Otto knew that there was going to be trouble and that he couldn't leave his new acquaintance in the lurch. He had to help him. He rose from his cover, frantically fumbling with the little pistol, taped to the inside of his right thigh, so that a casual observer might have thought as he groped inside his open flies that the handsome young man stumbling down the road was about to commit an act of gross indecency, instead of one which is regarded in military circles as 'above and beyond the call of normal duty'.

Now the tramp was on his feet, gaze fixed warily on the muzzle of the border-guard's rifle, which was only a metre away from his skinny stomach, while the cop continued to bellow at him. Suddenly he acted. He kicked hard. The gravel at his feet shot up into the man's crimson face and momentarily blinded him. The next instant Ami had turned and was pelting down the road towards Otto, who had now finally freed the little pistol, arms and legs flailing for all they were worth.

Behind him the border-guard shook his head like an enraged bull and lifted the rifle to his shoulder, ignoring the protests of the soldiers, their grins gone now. '*Halt!*' he cried thickly. '*Halt!*'

Otto swallowed hard. Would the flying tramp stop? But Ami had no intention of obeying the cop's command. He tucked his head into his skinny shoulders, as if ducking beneath heavy rain, and kept on running.

Otto flung a last glance at the cop's face. He recognised that hardening of the jaw and the whitening of the hand grasping the rifle instantly. The man was going to fire, and at that range he couldn't miss. He groaned hard. There was nothing for it. He would have to do it again! He raised the pistol and aimed at the cop's big knee, just above the shining leather of the man's boot. I hope this pea-shooter doesn't fire high, he said to himself through gritted teeth, otherwise your missus is going to have good grounds for divorce, copper. Next instant he pulled the trigger.

The pistol jerked in his hand.

'*Ouch!*' the big cop dropped his rifle to the gravel with a yelp of agony and started hopping around on one leg, hands clasped tightly to his shattered knee comically, a hurt look on his face like someone at a football match, appealing to the referee and crowd that he had been unfairly kicked, while behind him the soldiers scattered for cover or ran for their positions, crying in sudden panic. *'C'est la guerre . . . on attaque . . . aux armes, camrades. . . !'*

Next instant Otto and Ami were running for their lives back into the trees from whence they had come, slugs cutting the air all around them, and the big cop continued to hop around on one foot, making little miserable moaning sounds.

'A big shitting Calvinist cop,' Ami said after handing back the paper with the information about the Losheim Bridge pencilled upon it. 'Unreformed church, of course. They're the worse. They don't even drink coffee, cos they think it's sinful. Religious maniac,' he continued bitterly, as they moved off again, steadily progressing ever deeper into the Ardennes forest. 'The big shit wanted the sergeant of the guard to put me in the cooler on account of I was corrupting the young soldiers with my dirty photos' he sniffed scornfully. 'Corrupt that lot of hairy-arsed wankers! Biggest bunch of brothel-bashers, I've ever seen – and that's saying a lot! . . . Grr, I hope he gets his dick caught in the wringer next wash-day!'

'Next wash-day, he'll still be in dock, I shouldn't wonder,' Otto said sourly and changing the subject, added, 'How far to the frontier now, Ami?'

'Not more than a kilometre, comrade. Don't worry, old Ami won't let you down. Thirty minutes at the most and I'll have you safely back in your Fatherland.'

Otto grinned. 'You're a card, Ami.'

'So they tell me.'

'But listen, what about you? Will you be safe? I mean that cop won't forget your face.'

'Don't you worry about me, comrade,' Ami said confidently. 'I've got one of those faces about which you can say – once seen, forgotten for ever.' He grinned up at Otto, whose face glistened with sweat at the effort demanded by the long uphill climb through the thick firs. 'Worry about yourself because you know what all this lark's about, don't yer, the details of the bridges and that?'

Otto feigned stupidity. 'Not really,' he answered.

'Come off it, comrade. You and me weren't born yesterday. There's gonna be fighting here, lots of it: the frontier'll run with blood.'

'Sounds a bit far-fetched,' Otto said purposefully non-committal.

'Don't!' Ami said stubbornly. 'In my mind's eye I can see the stiffs stretched out on every metre of ground we're stepping on now.' He shuddered violently, his wizened little face suddenly very pale, and at his side, Otto did the same. At that moment he believed the tramp. The frontier would run with blood.

'Don't say things like that,' he said thickly.

Ami said nothing and in silence they marched on.

In years to come Otto would think of his companion's words that November day in 1939 for Ami had been both wrong and right. In 1940 when the German Army did move finally across it, they did so with hardly a casualty, thanks to the little tramp's efforts. Four years later, after the disastrous Ardennes offensive, Ami's prediction was vindicated, and a ragged, starving Otto fled across that frontier, running across a carpet of bloody corpses.

'"D",' Ami explained, cleaning the green moss off the little border stone, 'stands for *Deutschland* . . . and here "B" for *Belgique*.' He straightened up and smiled at Otto. 'Told yer Ami'd be able to do it, didn't I?'

'Do you mean this is the frontier?'

Ami nodded.

'Don't look much, does it?' Otto commented, staring across the field into the Reich.

Ami laughed a little hollowly. 'Across there is as far away as the moon from the earth, really.'

'And what's that supposed to mean?'

Ami didn't answer directly. Instead he said, 'Listen,

comrade, why don't you just stay over here and become a gent-of-the road before it's too late? I'll see you all right. You're a decent sort of a bloke for – well you know what I mean? That shitting cop would have croaked me for good, if it hadn't been for you and that pop-gun of yourn.'

Otto did not answer for a moment, as if he were seriously considering the little tramp's offer, then finally he shook his head. 'Thanks Ami,' he said and he meant it. 'But I'm a German. For better or for worse, I'll have to stick with my own folk.'

Ami nodded his understanding and stuck out his hand. 'Have it your way, and remember when you're *Gauleiter* of Paris, think of old Ami, child of the frontier. I could do a good chicken-dinner with all the trimmings.'

'I won't forget.'

They shook hands solemnly and then Otto stretched out his right leg beyond the little stone with its 'B' and 'D' and stepped into Germany. Ami turned and stumped off without another word. Five minutes later he had vanished into the forest. Otto never saw the 'child of the frontier' again.

EIGHT

For the new *Sonderfuhrer* Otto Stahl* the winter of 1939–40 passed uneventfully enough in that remote spy-school near the little town of Duren. The only incidents of any moment which disturbed the crazy peace of the *Abwehr* training school were the heavy snows of December and January, the worst for twenty years in the Eifel; they were so bad that they blocked the little winding hilly road to Duren for over two weeks and the Count now took to visiting the school by means of a snow-white Fieseler Storch, which he had somehow organised in that mysterious manner of his.

'Leaflet-dropping,' he explained when Otto once queried him about his latest acquisition. 'Important means of subverting the enemy, you know.' For some reason his gaze could not meet Otto's, though at the time the young *Sonderfuhrer* paid little attention to the fact.

'I can imagine, Meadow,' he had sniffed, 'what any sensible Frog or Tommy is going to do when he gets one of those leaflets in his hands.'

The Count had been in no way offended. 'Perhaps you are right, Otto. They would be a little gentler on the jolly old rump than the usual issue Army latrine paper.'

Apart from the snow and the Count's new aeroplane, the only event at the spy-school to excite any attention

* Special Leader, a non-military rank created for civilians serving in the Army in certain special functions, such as interpreter, teacher, spy-hunter, etc.

was the weekly discussions by that crazy staff of impossible new methods of 'liquidating' the enemy, as they always phrased it.

'Poisoned barbed wire,' someone would suggest as they gathered in the big mess, with the wood crackling merrily in the ceiling-high green-tiled stoves which heated the place, and the snow falling in solid white sheets outside. 'You could scratch yourself on it and die in sheer agony within the hour.'

'What's the poison?' someone else would ask.

'Curare.'

'Ah,' there'd be a knowing murmur from the rest. 'South American stuff, eh.' And they would be launched on an interminable crazy discussion of the Matto Grosso and the lost treasures of Montezuma. Another time someone would remark with apparent casualness. 'It has occurred to me that migrating birds are the only individuals who could enter French territory without exciting suspicion.'

'Tiny bombs tied around their necks?' one of the crazy men would start the ball rolling eagerly.

'No, certain hideous disease germs would be better,' there'd be a counter-suggestion. And so it would go on until it was realised that there were no bird-migrations in Western Europe in the dead of winter.

In the end Otto gave up going after a long winter's afternoon discussing Brass Eggs's 'explosive horse-apple', a simulated piece of horseshit, filled with TNT, which according to him would blow the foot off any enemy soldier foolish enough to step into it. Twice he protested that no one in his right mind stepped into horseshit, not even idiot Frog soldiers, and twice his protests were overruled by the others with cries that the French were intoxicated all the time, everyone knew that, and besides they were peasants for the most part and had this mythical attachment to the soil – and shit.

Sonderfuhrer Stahl resigned from the 'Lethal Secret Weapons Committee', as it was called, without regret and concentrated on his duties, which were not particularly onerous: training a succession of seedy, clumsy, sullen and sometimes definitely shady young men who purportedly were volunteers for the dangerous profession of spy, but who, Otto suspected, were culled from the local jails of the Eifel. Invariably he wrote on their confidential reports to Gertie that they were unfit for their chosen profession, hoping to spare their necks that way, but when he discovered that the reports never went any further and that Gertie was using them, and anything else he could lay his hands on, as fuel for the greenhouse in which he was trying to develop a new cross-strain of the South American fly-eating orchid that would eat human flesh – 'Imagine, *Sonderfuhrer*, plant one of those in General Gamelin's* conservatory and – snap – *his arm is off*! That would bring a rapid halt to the French war-machine' – he gave up. Once a week, weather permitting, Otto would go to Duren in the company truck to fetch 'supplies'. In reality he used the afternoon to make love to his new mistress, a flighty blonde in her mid-thirties, who was given to easy tears and quick passions and maintained that she was the wife of a general serving in Poland. Otto didn't believe her until one afternoon, they were interrupted in the middle of their love-making by a brass band playing outside her bedroom window, and she started up, crying, 'Oh shit, it's my birthday, the General's got the local band to play me a few airs by way of a present, the silly sod! You'd think he'd know I've better things to do.'

So they had to wait impatiently while the local volunteer fire-brigade band ground its way through a selection of Lehar, Strauss, and naturally Wagner, idly tossing burning cigarette-ends into the mouth of the souzaphone.

Then when the band had shuffled off, fumbling their way through the inevitable '*muss i denn zum staedele hinaus*', she had turned to him urgently and cried in

* Commander of the French Army.

dismay at the effect the horrible music had had upon him, 'Oh, look, my present's vanished!'

But as February 1940 began to give way to March, Otto returning from his pleasant afternoons in Duren could see that the Eifel forests and villages were beginning to fill up with new troops rapidly. There were tanks, trucks, cannon and soldiers everywhere, packed into the white-painted cottages, grouped round the slate-roofed, onion-towered baroque churches, crowded into the half-timbered farmhouses where both humans and animals slept under the same dark thatched roof and the whole house stank of boiled white cabbage and animal droppings.

Once he had to stop while a column of 75mm cannon were manhandled into position at the side of the road by sweating angry soldiers, with others following them up, armed with twigs and farm brooms to sweep away the tell-tale tracks in the snow. At night, too, low-flying fighters flew from dusk to dawn to mask the rattle of tanks moving up ever closer to what would soon be the new front, making the darkness hideous with their snarling, roaring engines.

The school started to fill up too with a new type of trainee; men from the Brandenburg Regiment stationed in Duren, 'come here,' as Gertie said in his welcoming address, 'to receive the final polish, from teachers who themselves have learnt their trade in the field'.

They were a strange bunch of individuals of all trades and professions, many of whom spoke German with a strong accent, recruited obviously from the many overseas Germans who had been caught in the Reich by the outbreak of the war and had been conscripted in Father Christmas's special commandos on account of their knowledge of foreign tongues and foreign places. A surprising number of them, Otto discovered, came from South Africa and spoke Afrikaans among themselves, including a dusky-skinned young man from Windhoek, who was always cold and was inclined to break up the furniture to make a fire on the floor of his room over which he grilled worms, and once even a hedgehog he had found dead on the road outside.

Jokingly Otto had suggested that the presence of so many 'South Africans', as the recruits were called by the staff, indicated that the Fuhrer intended to launch a blitzkrieg against the Dark Continent next. But his suggestion was taken seriously by Gertie and for a couple of weeks the Lethal Secret Weapons Committee met in the stifling heat of the Commandant's greenhouse, brushing off the importunings of the fly-eating orchids and sweating heavily in their winter uniforms as a kind of acclimatisation for the coming campaign.

Now on his weekly visits to the school, the 'Flying Fool', as the Brandenburgers called the Count, who had somehow managed to obtain a pilot's licence and invariably scared the pants off them as he came winging down at tree-top height to make his terrible, bumpy landings on the lawn, looked increasingly more worried as March gave way to April and the warlike preparations at the frontier continued at high speed.

Wrongly, as he discovered later, Otto assumed that the Count's worried appearance had something to do with the coming offensive in the West; but that spring the Count was playing his mysterious game with his cards held closely to his chest and Otto got little out of the flamboyant aristocrat, save enigmatic remarks such as, 'The longer I study men, Otto, the more I like dogs. Frederick the Great, you know?' followed by heavy sighs, as if the cares of the world weighed down on his shoulders.

Now, too, the Count started to take a great deal of interest in the special weapons being developed for use by the Brandenburgers, especially the silenced carbine that was being tested at that particular time. Twice Otto came across the heavy-built aristocrat lying full length on the range, firing the secret weapon at the butts, though Otto was amused to see that he had attached the school's portable electric generator to the electric blanket upon which he lay.

'I doubt if the Greater German Army will provide you with an electric blanket in the field, Meadow, eh?' he had quipped. But his sally had brought no answering smile from the Count. Indeed his face had assumed that tragic 'man-of-destiny' look that Otto had noted on it before and he had replied sombrely, 'I must take the greatest care of myself, Otto,' and had added for some mysterious reason known only to himself, '*especially now!*'

On the morning of 10 April 1940, the school was startled by the announcement over the 'People's Receiver', lodged in the mess, that the Fuhrer had gone to the aid of little Denmark, which had been attacked by the perfidious English in their usual treacherous fashion. An hour later the radio broadcast the same statement about Norway, though this time the speaker announced threateningly that if the Norwegians rejected the hand of friendship offered to them so nobly by the Fuhrer, he would be forced to employ the 'severest and most relentless means to crush the ingrates'.

'It is unbelievable, isn't it, that people could be so ungrateful?' Gertie had commented and smoothed down his skirt, which he had immediately donned after the first announcement ('in case we have to go into action at once. One can't be too prepared'). Now things began to move swiftly. The *Sitzkrieg** in the West was over at last and now the air-waves and the newspapers were full of battles in strange places with tongue-twisting names in the far north of Norway. In spite of himself, Otto became an addict, glued to the radio, listening to accounts of bitter fighting in Narvik and Bergen and the sea-battles off the Arctic coast, in which it was clear that the Tommies had given the *Kriegsmarine* a bloody nose; even Goebbels' Propaganda Ministry could not quite conceal that fact. He even neglected his weekly visits to the blonde in Duren and when he did visit her, she complained bitterly that he was letting the 'shitting

* The German equivalent of 'phoney war'.

war' get in the way 'of really important things, like fucking'.

It was in the third week of that April that Father Christmas, the white-haired, little Admiral who headed the *Abwehr*, made a surprise appearance at the spy-school. An hour later the Count's plane came roaring in at roof-top height too, taking with it several tiles and so shocking the dusky 'South African' that he swallowed one of his horrible, half-grilled worms in a sudden frightened gulp. That afternoon the surprise visit of Father Christmas and his chief subordinate seemed to be a pure coincidence. Later he was to realise that it had all been planned.

Thus it was that he could not make much sense out of the fragments of conversation he chanced to overhear through the window of the room in which the two spy-masters met, which was open on account of its being an unusually warm day for April.

'The pretext,' the Admiral was saying, 'that he is off to visit Field Marshal von Mackensen up in Hamburg . . . It's his ninetieth birthday . . . Half-way there, somewhere around Celle perhaps, the special train will be switched on to the line heading south. They'll reach Munster . . .'

At that moment one of the low-flying fighters had zoomed in low over the house, the snarl of its engine drowning the little Admiral's words so that Otto had not been able to make out which of the several towns named 'Munster' in Germany the Admiral meant.

'There will be a motor cavalcade waiting for him there at the station to escort him to the Mountain-nest.' The Admiral laughed scornfully, 'What a hopeless romantic he is! In my time,' he exclaimed, 'a serious commander would never have picked a name like that for his HQ.'

'And Wolf for his own code-name,' Count von der Weide said equally contemptuously. 'Typical petit-bourgeois!'

Otto frowned. '*Wolf!*' Hadn't the Count once said that was the Fuhrer's code-name? Of course, he had. The two spy-masters were talking about Hitler.

'At all events, you can be sure that he'll be there by five that afternoon. At this time of the year,' the Admiral said, 'that should give you two good hours of light still.'

'Yes, that would be about it,' Otto heard the Count say but there was no overhearing the note of fear in his voice.

Then the window was shut with a bang and Otto was left, lying in the grass, with the flies buzzing lazily all around him, the sunrays playing on his pleasantly flushed face, his brow creased in a worried frown. 'What does Meadow still need two good hours of light for?' he asked himself thoughtfully. And why had the Count sounded so scared? What was going on?

The answer to those very puzzling questions, Otto was able to reconstruct only much later, long after the war had been lost and all of the principal actors had died a violent death. He knew there were loopholes in his reconstruction and all he really knew of the event was that on the evening of 8 May 1940 Count von der Weide smashed his bright-white plane into the side of the spy-school and had come staggering out of the smoking wreckage, crying, 'Everyone to the front . . . everyone to the front!' like a crazy man before passing out in Gertie's arms. He was, however, later able to be fairly satisfied that the strange events of that May must have taken place something like this . . .

NINE

It had not been a good day for Adolf Hitler.

The deception with the train had gone well enough and, during a small stop-over near Hanover, his Chief Meteorologist Diesing predicted good weather for 10 May, the day the *Wehrmacht* would march westwards. Pleased, Hitler had awarded the weatherman a gold watch. But when his train, code-named 'Amerika' for some reason that no one in his entourage could fathom, reached Aachen, the border city was shrouded in thick fog. From thence to Euskirchen, where the car entourage had been waiting, it had been fog all the way.

Now that he was at last in his HQ, a bunker installation blasted out of a wooded mountaintop especially for the great offensive, the fog had lifted. But the damage had already been done. His nerves and his unruly stomach had combined to give him one of his usual attacks.

As always he had taken his strong laxative because he had a horror of getting fat. 'A leader must be lean and tough as a wolf,' he always proclaimed. Half an hour later, the laxative had been followed by opium pills to quell the rumbles and pains in his abdomen, and thereafter a series of other medicines prescribed by his owl-faced personal doctor, Dr Theo Morell. But nothing seemed able to stop his meteorism this evening; and Linge, Hitler's tall solemn body-servant, was getting the full benefit of it, crowded together as the two men were in that little room. On the radio, which Linge had switched on to drown the painful, embarrassing noises the Fuhrer made at regular intervals, a child was reciting the new grace being introduced into the city of Cologne in a Rhenish sing-song:

'Fuhrer, my Fuhrer, bequeathed to me by the Lord . . . Protect and preserve me as long as I live . . . Thou hast rescued Germany from deepest distress . . . Abide this long with me, foresake me not . . . Fuhrer, my Fuhrer, my faith and my light. Heil my Fuhrer.'

Unknown to the little girl, her Fuhrer punctuated each line of her plaintive invocation with a ripe fart, raising his booted right leg to facilitate the process, while behind him Linge grew progressively paler as the room filled up with the noxious gas. Hitler's attack of meteorism was reaching its crescendo.

In the end the Fuhrer decided that the odour of rotten eggs was too much even for him, although he had lived with it these forty-odd years.

'I think I'll just go outside on the terrace, Linge,' he announced, 'and get a breath of . . . er . . . fresh air.'

'*Jawohl, mein Fuhrer,*' Linge said in his funereal voice. Linge breathed a gasp of relief as the Fuhrer limped outside, still farting strongly, and grabbed for the flask of strong eau-de-cologne which he kept concealed in his sleeve specially for this particular eventuality. With shaking fingers he unscrewed the cap and thrust the neck into each nostril in turn, knowing that this was the only way to drown the awful stench and cure his dizziness. His high rank of colonel in the SS did not justify the torture the Fuhrer submitted him to, he told himself yet once again. Sometimes he felt he would be happier at the front. At least there, they wouldn't employ poison gas.

Count von der Weide's heart leapt. It was him. There was no mistaking that figure who had suddenly appeared on the terrace outside the low-lying bunker, hopping about, as if he were doing some strange little polka. It was Hitler all right!

Father Christmas and the other conspirators in the top ranks of the *Abwehr* and *Wehrmacht* had been attempting to 'dispense with' (the euphemism the aristocratic plotters preferred to use) the Fuhrer for some twelve months now. But time and time again their carefully laid plans had gone askew.

There had been the disgruntled SS-man, whom they had bribed to put a bomb under his Hitler's rostum at *Hofbrauhaus* just before the Fuhrer was due to make his annual speech to the old guard of the Munich branch of the Party. But at the crucial moment when he should have planted the bomb and disappeared with his forged passport and wallet-full of Swiss francs over the border, he had been taken short by an attack of diarrhoea. Bolting for the pub's toilet, he had been inadvertently locked in by a comrade, bomb still in his tunic pocket.

There had been another bomb, complete with time-fuse, concealed in a big bunch of red roses and thrust at the Fuhrer's car by what appeared to be a gushing enthusiastic fat lady (it was an *Abwehr* agent in disguise). It was planned that the thing would explode once it was placed in a vase in the Fuhrer's sitting-room in the Berghof refuge, which he called home. It never reached that destination. Apparently the black-uniformed bodyguard who intercepted it from the 'fat lady' placed it on the new grave of his mother-in-law in the local cemetery – obviously in an attempt to save money for flowers – where it exploded, scattering bits of his unlamented mother-in-law all over the place. The affair caused some surprise in family circles, but it was generally agreed among the relatives that it was a fate the late, unlamented had richly deserved.

And then there had been an attempt in the summer of 1939 to pump poison gas into the new Reichschancellery's air-conditioning system by a chimney-sweep bribed to secret the containers on the roof. But again their plan had failed. The attempt had backfired for some inexplicable reason and the gas had flooded into the Berlin sky. All that day blackbirds and sparrows had kept falling off the roofs of the government district to splatter on the streets below like black turds; and those of the officials who had enjoyed a classical education talked meaningfully of 'evil omens'.

But now after so many failures, the Count, prone in the smelly drainage pipe, peering through the opening, partly covered by ferns, knew he couldn't miss. This time Adolf Hitler, the hated tyrant, would not escape his fate!

The Count tensed. That well-known, pudgy face with that ridiculous lock of hair hanging down across the narrow forehead, swung into the bright circle of calibrated glass. He brought the silenced carbine down. His sight wavered over Hitler's Iron Cross and then up a little, to his breast pocket.

The Count checked his breath. This was a historic moment. At last the world would know soon that he really was a man-of-destiny; he would go down in the history books as the noble hero who had slain that evil genius. He took first pressure and then almost immediately, second. The trigger clicked home.

Nothing happened!

No familiar slap against his shoulder, whiff of acrid burnt cordite, with eight hundred metres away, Hitler reeling against the wall, clutching at his shattered heart.

He tried again.

Again nothing!

The sweat pouring down his forehead in thick opaque beads, legs twitching badly as he lay there, his heart racing furiously, he took careful aim. First pressure . . . Second pressure . . . Almost lovingly he eased the trigger the full length.

Nothing!

'Heaven, arse and cloudburst!' he cursed with surprising, unusual profanity for him. He had a damned stoppage!

Hurriedly he crawled out of his hiding-place and broke open the magazine. With shaking fingers he drew out the special cartridges and flung them in the general direction of the Fuhrer, as if he were attempting to stone the tyrant to death. A damned bullet was jammed in the breech. That was why the Brandenburgers' carbine wouldn't fire!

'Oh, this is just too much!' he cried, exasperated beyond measure that after all this planning, his assassination attempt had failed too, and dashed the rifle against the pipe.

The rifle exploded and gave him such a shock that he almost fell over. A bullet went winging across the valley towards the bunker and the lone figure standing on the terrace. But abruptly panicked, the Count did not wait to see if he had hit its target. He fled, blundering wildly through the thick undergrowth, heading for the place where he had hidden his plane, leaving the tell-tale carbine behind him.

Hitler, his face contorted with agony, raised his right knee level with his murderously rumbling, tormented stomach, and loosed off a tremendous fart that exploded like a clap of thunder and brought immediate relief.

Above him, just where his head had been a moment before, a hole appeared surprisingly enough in the concrete, spreading outwards in little ripples of cracked stucco.

Hitler stared at it in wonder. '*Gott im Himmel!*' he said to himself. 'I really must order Doctor Morell to reduce the strength of those little pills of his.' Then still sighing with relief that his stomach cramps seemed to be over for the time being, he passed inside the bunker once more to recommence the task of conquering the world.

TEN

'Evacuate the school!' Gertie cried to the startled staff crowding in on him. 'To the front!'

'What?' Otto gasped. Like the others he had come here to find out what had happened to the Count; he had not expected this startling development. 'What did you say, Major?'

'Meadow has just brought us our new orders from Father Christmas. There has been an attempt on the Fuhrer's life. Obviously agents of perfidious Albion at work again. That devil with the umbrella is behind it all, I'll be bound,' the Commandant snorted in red-faced anger. 'But Providence has intervened yet once again. *Gott mit uns!*'

'*Santa Maria!*' Hirsch exclaimed solemnly and crossed himself, dark Jewish eyes turned upwards to heaven, burning with fervent piety. 'Thank God!'

There was a murmur of 'thank Gods' from all around.

Angrily Otto pushed the pious idiots out of the way to confront Gertie, who for some reason was wearing a Red Cross nurse's uniform, one salmon-pink bloomer-leg hanging down from beneath the white apron.

'What's the fact that there's been an attempt on the Fuhrer's life got to do with our being sent to the front?' he demanded.

'I don't know exactly. Meadow was too weak. But my guess is that the Fuhrer's plans have been betrayed and that we of the *Abwehr* are needed up there to save the offensive.'

'But I'm a civilian,' Otto objected. 'I can't fight . . . it's illegal.'

Gertie looked at Otto's flushed face haughtily. 'As of today, *Sonderfuhrer* Stahl,' he said with biting contempt, tugging up his bloomers as he did so, 'there are no soldiers or civilians. The Fatherland is in great peril. As of today, there are just *Germans*!' And with that he turned and stalked away, as if his contemptuous statement had solved everything, leaving Otto to stare at his fat, short-skirted bottom in absolute bewilderment.

While the Brandenburgers ran to and fro outside, excitedly packing their special gear and crying at regular intervals, 'To the front!,' and in their rooms the staff busily arranged their private world, crazy as it was, the Count looked at himself in the mirror for a long time, adjusting and re-adjusting the bloodstained bandage around his head until it sat at a suitably heroic attitude.

For a while he forgot the danger, as he fell yet once again in love with his face. His eyes were dark and enormous and seemed to him tragic like those of a man bound to suffer some heroic fate. They were the eyes of a man who could not avoid his allotted destiny, however hard and bitter that destiny might be.

The sound of the waiting Maps lighting his blowtorch returned him to the present and the need for urgent action.

Of course Father Christmas would disown him, he realised that and was not hurt by the realisation. The conspiracy must go on. If Canaris were questioned by the Gestapo, he would deny all knowledge of the affair. For the time being, therefore, he was on his own. Naturally the Gestapo would trace that damned special rifle to the Brandenburgers, and from their barracks in Duren, the trail would lead here to the spy-school. Hence all evidence that might incriminate him and the others had to be destroyed. But that wasn't enough. They would have to indulge in a 'flight to the front', as they had once called it as young officers in another war.

In the confusion of the new front in the West, especially that section of it allotted to the Brandenburgers, all traces could be eradicated. All of them would have to go, even Otto. No one could be left behind to be questioned by the Gestapo bloodhounds, in particular, the crazy staff. God only knew what would come out if they started blabbing!

Once the offensive started up there in Holland, they would come back as heroes or they wouldn't come back at all. And in the last resort, one could always desert to the enemy. One way or other, the immediate problem would be solved.

He straightened up and stared at the waiting Maps. 'Listen,' he said, his voice filled with new hope and purpose, 'you're right. The whole place is infested with them.'

Maps's crazy eyes narrowed. 'Little green swine,' he whispered, tossing a hasty glance to left and right, as if they might be overheard, 'With metallic ears like large antennae?' He raised one hand, fingers outstretched and waggled it behind his ear.

The Count swallowed. 'Yes, that's them.'

'I knew you'd come to my way of thinking in the end, Meadow!' Maps said triumphantly. 'When do I start burning them?' He lifted the hissing blow-torch and started to regulate the control.

'No time for that,' the Count snapped. 'Besides there are too many of them. No friend, radical situations require radical solutions. Blow . . .'

'Yes,' Maps hung open-mouthed on his every word. 'Yes . . . yes?'

'Blow the whole place up! Raze it to the ground! Leave no stone standing!' the Count cried dramatically. 'We must eradicate the evil green swine – *once and for all*!' Spontaneously an exuberant Maps burst into '*Deutschland uber alles*'.

Thus as that strange motley crowd of Brandenburgers and crazy men from the *Abwehr* left their remote fastness for the last time, a singing Maps blew up building after building, crying after every fresh explosion, 'How do you like that, you filthy green swine?'

But in the trucks filing slowly down the narrow country roads northwards towards the Dutch frontier and what lay ahead for their occupants there, there was no singing.

Instead the men slumped in gloomy reverie, their eyes closed, all energy and enthusiasm sped as quickly as they had come, each man preoccupied with his own pessimistic thoughts, even the most crazy of them. All were abruptly sobered by the terrible knowledge that Mars had summoned them at last.

They were going to war. Somewhere soon that greedy monster with his blood-red dripping maws would be waiting for them. *How many of them would escape?*

THREE : OTTO BECOMES A HERO
(FOR A WHILE)

'He, the trained spy, had walked into the trap
For a bogus guide, seduced with the old tricks.'

W. H. Auden

ONE

'Gentlemen,' the Count announced in that new sharp, clipped military style of his, 'the situation is serious but not impossible.'

There was a murmur of agreement from the assembled spy-school staff, grouped around him in the gloomy gothic hall of the border castle which the Count had high-handedly requisitioned the previous day 'in the name of the Wehrmacht'. Now that they all knew 'X-hour' would take place on the night of 9–10 May, they wore uniforms complete with steel helmet and were festooned with pistols, spare ammunition clips, smoke grenades and stick-bombs. Even Otto had decided it was safer to wear a helmet, for he reasoned that if he had to go into action with the idiots of the spy-school, it might save him from a bullet in the head from his own side.

Octavio Hirsch was the only exception. His head bore what appeared to be a khaki solar topee, decorated with the feather-bush of the *Bersaglieri* that drooped down the side of his face and onto his skinny right shoulder so that it looked as if he had a multi-coloured, if somewhat scraggy, parrot roosting there.

'It will not be easy, gentlemen,' the Count continued. 'But then we of the *Abwehr* have never wanted it that way.'

'Here, here,' they agreed solemnly, and the Count gave them one of his new martial stares and tried to forget the tight corset which gave him the requisite narrow waist that went with the elegant cavalry officer's uniform he now wore.

'Our task?' He answered his own question. 'The capture of the bridges across the Meuse-Waal Canal at Gennep and Heuem . . . In addition, the three Maastricht bridges. Clear?' he barked.

'*Klar, Herr Oberst*,' they replied dutifully.

Otto shook his head in mock wonder. Overnight the spy-school cretins had taken to playing soldiers, as if it were all a great game. God knows what they would be like when the real thing started!

'Naturally, all five bridges are defended by Dutch infantry. There will be barbed wire and probably mines too. And we cannot expect the Dutch to stand by tamely while we capture their bridges, what?' He beamed at them in a brisk military manner.

There were several chuckles and Gertie said, 'Not on, sir.'

'Of course they will make an attempt to defend them and failing that, they will blow them up. However,' he tapped the side of his long nose and winked solemnly at them, 'we of the *Abwehr* are not in intelligence for nothing. Brain has always triumphed over brute force, has it not, gentlemen?'

There was a rumble of agreement and Brass Eggs, the homosexual unarmed combat expert, looked disappointed, as if he had half-expected to tackle the enemy bare-handed, grabbing from testicle to testicle in an attempt to knock out the defenders.

'You have all enjoyed a classical education, gentlemen,' the Count continued, 'and know the tale of the Trojan Horse.' 'Isn't that the name of a brand of Turkish fag?' Otto said maliciously, trying to bring this bunch of fools and cretins back down to earth.

The Count ignored him, as did the others. Now they were hanging on the aristocrat's words and Otto could see that he and they were really enjoying themselves. 'So we have created a little Trojan Horse of our own,' the

Count went on. He nodded to Gertie. '*Major Haase, bitte.*'

Haase swung round smartly and marched to the big oaken door. He opened it with difficulty and, red-faced with the sudden exertion, barked in heavily-accented Dutch, '*Als t u blieft, soldaaten!*' There was the sudden sound of marching feet and Haase intoned the cadence solemnly in Dutch '*een, twi, drie!*' as the 'South Africans' stamped into the big hall, each man dressed in a green Dutch Army uniform, complete with puttees, and started to mark time noisily in front of the astonished staff with what looked like black ink dripping down from their helmets onto their martially set faces.

'*Dank u wel!*' the Count said in Dutch, his brow furrowed against the racket the heavy ammunition boots made on the stone floor, and then in German, 'Please, would you stop it. My head!' He touched his bandaged head under the rakishly tilted cavalry officer's cap tenderly.

The 'South Africans' stumbled to a ragged halt and stood there at attention, obviously embarrassed by the black drops which dripped persistently from their helmets.

'It's the helmets,' the Count explained. 'Our agents stole the uniforms, the boots, even the puttees, everything. The only thing they forgot were the helmets. Our workshops had to make them of plywood, but obviously the dye isn't what it should be. That rain outside has had its effect.' He smiled winningly. 'No matter. Our beloved Fuhrer has promised us good weather, with sunshine, for X-hour – and our Fuhrer is never wrong.'

'Here, here!' they cried.

Now it dawned on Otto why he had been assigned to steal the Belgian uniforms the year before. The *Abwehr* had intended all along to capture the border in Holland and Belgium by subterfuge and not force. The Count's next words confirmed his sudden realisation. 'Gentlemen,' he announced, one hand outstretched towards the embarrassed 'South Africans' with an expansive gesture like a clothes salesman displaying the latest fashions, 'these pseudo-Dutchmen are going to be our Trojan Horse.'

There was a burst of delighted clapping.

Swiftly and confidently, his fear and frustration at the failure of the assassination attempt forgotten now, delighted in his new role as a leader of men, the Count outlined his plan, covering in some detail each of the officers' present place in it. Crazy men that they were, they beamed when it came to each of their turns, squaring their shoulders martially and staring hard-eyed and fierce at some distant horizon.

Then it was the turn of Octavio Hirsch and Otto.

For a few moments Otto was struck speechless by the sheer improbability of the Count's intentions, then finally he found his voice and blurted out, 'But I'm a shitting civilian, Meadow! And that little spaghetti-eater,' he indicated a proud Hirsch with a shaking finger (for Otto too had come to accept the portly little Jew's feigned Italian origin), 'is so cracked in the upper storey, he doesn't know enough to come out of the shitting rain!'

'*Corragio*, Otto!' Hirsch cried boldly. 'We can only die once!'

'Oh shut up, you stupid Italian fart!' Otto cried, beside himself with rage and frustration.

The Count strode forward and laid a fatherly hand on the younger man's shaking shoulder. 'Keep your nerve, my boy,' he said, face set in its new heroic, leader-of-men mould. 'I know well the strain of going over the top for the first time. *My God*, do I not! It is understandable. But it is a fear that we all have and we all overcome, *nicht wahr, meine Herren*?' There was a murmur of agreement from the rest and Brass Eggs started making fierce little milking movements with both hands, as if he could already visualise himself ripping off Dutch testicles.

'Don't worry, Otto,' the Count said and squeezed the other man's shoulder hard. 'If the worst comes to the worst, I shall be there to support you.'

'What?'

'Yes,' the Count said with a tight military smile, 'I am going with your group.'

Otto groaned. 'Now I know it's going to be a complete balls-up,' he moaned and gave up.

TWO

Just before dawn on the morning of 10 May 1940, an oddly assorted group of Dutch soldiers, armed with fixed bayonets, and what seemed to be a bunch of unarmed, sullen German infantrymen, appeared from the pre-dawn ground haze at the lock-bridge near the little frontier town of Gennep.

The sentries of the Dutch 26th Infantry Regiment, guarding the key bridge, watched carefully from their slit trenches, as the group came ever closer. All of them knew that an alert had been called for that morning. All night long there had been false alarms that the great German invasion had already started and rumours that the *Moffen* had been dropping paratroops behind the Dutch lines had flown from hole to hole more than once that night. The Germans appeared to be the usual deserters – all winter they had been coming over to neutral Holland and begging for asylum – and they were under Dutch guard. Still the men of the 26th Infantry were wary; they knew they were not supposed to take any chances.

Thus when the group came to within fifty metres of the first 26th position, the soldier there sprang out of his hole, rifle levelled and commanded the men to halt. They did so obediently and waited for further orders.

'Advance one and be recognised!' the sentry commanded, voice firm, bayonetted rifle at his hip and at the ready, while behind him the guard-commander turned the portable searchlight on the waiting man.

Smartly a man wearing the stars of a senior sergeant on his shoulder stepped up to the sentry, papers at the ready. Hastily the sentry took his eyes off one of the escort, who seemed to have a worm dangling out of the side of his mouth, and told himself that it had been a trick of the light. He checked the senior sergeant's papers which were perfectly in order and the NCO explained that he commanded a patrol which had bumped into the Germans in the act of throwing away their weapons. They were the usual *Moffen* deserters.

'They don't say much, do they,' the sentry said and signalled to the men behind to start lowering the lock-bridge so that the deserters and their escort could pass over.

'*Zwijgen als een mof*,' the senior sergeant quipped, as the bridge began to creak down.*

Now the prisoners started to march sullenly across the bridge, heading for the cages that were supposed to lie to the rear, deeper in Holland. 'Miserable bunch of shits,' the sentry said to the NCO, who was eyeing his captives sternly. 'Come over here now and sit on their fat German arses eating all our butter and cheese. You'd think they'd only be too happy to get their balls shot off for their beloved Fuhrer.'

The NCO grunted something.

'Heil Hitler!' the sentry said mockingly at one prisoner who bore what seemed, in that half-light, a parrot on his skinny shoulder, and gave a loud fart.

The deserter dropped his head as if embarrassed.

Now the whole group had crossed the narrow stretch of water and halted in front of the guard-commander, a big bluff NCO smoking a black cheroot, taking a puff and giving a thick smoker's cough at regular intervals.

Salutes were exchanged between him and the senior sergeant of the escort, while the deserters stared

* 'Silent as a grave' – a pun on the word 'mof' which can mean 'Jerry' as well as 'grave'.

around, blinking in the lights, obviously taking in the sights of the country which would soon be their prison. The guard-commander suggested he'd guide the senior sergeant and his captives to a barn where he could lodge them for the rest of the night until the HQ of the 26th Infantry Regiment passed on orders on what to do with the sullen *Moffen*.

The senior sergeant expressed his thanks and said it was an excellent idea. He swung round to his captives and bellowed '*Los!*'

But instead of the command making the prisoners shuffle off up the road to the barn, it galvanised them into violent action. Abruptly they were dragging machine-pistols and grenades from inside their tunics, darting forward like a well-trained football team, surging through the completely surprised Dutch sentries, while their former 'guards' were herding their first prisoners against the nearest wall, ripping off their pistol belts and ammunition, curtly ordering them in excellent if strangely accented Dutch to drop their rifles.

In a matter of minutes it was all over at the bridge itself and the Brandenburgers were already swarming down beneath it, slashing through the wires and cables that led to the explosive chamber, while above their prisoners watched them miserably, fists balled in angry impotent frustration.

'*Zwijgen als een mof,*' the grinning senior sergeant repeated his little phrase maliciously to the red-faced guard-commander and pulled the cheroot from between his gritted teeth to stick it triumphantly in his own mouth.

'No time for fraternising with the enemy,' the Count said severely, as he came striding imperiously across the bridge, his sabre clattering behind him, followed by Otto and the rest of the party. 'Can't you hear that?'

Somewhere in the gloom to the right of the bridge, a slow machine-gun had started to hammer.

'Dutch,' the Count snapped, as if he had spent all his

life recognising various types of machine-gun. 'Got to knock it out.'

Now green and red flares started to hiss into the pre-dawn sky from the general direction of the Dutch positions and it was clear even to a layman like Otto that the enemy were beginning to react, and react quickly.

For a moment the Count fumbled angrily with the hilt of his sabre and then he drew it out with a flourish, crying boldly, '*To the attack! . . . To the attack, soldiers . . . Hurrah!*'

'*Hurrah,*' a score of excited young men took up the cheer and abruptly the whole bunch of them were running forward to the sound of the machine-guns carrying a helpless Otto with them, crying plaintively, '*But I'm a shitting civilian!*' But now no one was listening to Otto Stahl.

Hirsch stumbled suddenly and his *Bersaglieri* helmet slipped absurdly to one side of his head.

'What's up?' Otto cried above the snap-and-crackle of the small arms fight that was increasing in intensity by the second. Somewhere there was the sound of high-speed motors racing in their direction.

'*Molto stupido,*' Hirsch gasped and his knees started to give way beneath him, his hands clutching his stomach.

Otto gulped with horror. Thick red stuff, which could only be blood was seeping through the little Jew's tightly clenched fingers. '*Octavio . . . Izzy!*' he cried in fearful alarm. Hirsch had been hit. He grabbed at him and gently lowered him to the ground. '*Oh veh, oh veh!*' Hirsch moaned in a thick Yiddish accent, as he writhed on the ground in his death agonies. '*Bei mir is alles . . .*' He didn't complete the sentence. Instead he looked up at a frantic Otto, his dark, pain-filled eyes sane for the first time since Otto had got to know him. '*Meschugge,*' he whispered and tapped his temple to make his meaning quite clear. 'A little Yid like Izzy

Hirsch dying for Hitler . . . *Total Meschugge!'* His eyeballs rolled upwards and suddenly his head lolled to one side.

It seemed to take Otto a long time to comprehend that Hirsch was dead and then abruptly something snapped within him and he was on his feet, carried away by that crazed blood-lust that attacks all men on a battlefield sooner or later, machine-pistol chattering frenetically at his side, racing towards the Dutch positions, screaming, '*You rotten cheesehead shits . . . you've murdered him! . . . Murdered little Hirsch in cold blood!'*

A soldier leapt from a trench and tried to bar his way. Otto's heavy boot lashed out. The Dutchman screamed and went reeling back, bright red blood jetting from his broken nose, spitting out broken teeth. To Otto's right, a pistol cracked. Some fool of an officer in full-dress uniform, complete with gleaming golden lanyard, stood there one hand on his fat hip, taking fresh aim as if he were on some peacetime range performing for the admiring ladies of the officers' corps.

Savagely Otto bared his teeth and pressed the trigger of his little mp. It chattered brutally at his hip. The front of the officer's uniform disappeared in a mess of bloody pulp. The pistol dropped from his nerveless fingers and his knees gave way beneath him, as if he had suddenly grown very tired. Otto ran on.

Still carried on by the impetus of his blood-rage, Otto was undismayed to see the three Dutch Army trucks flying down the little country road towards the bridge. Indeed he only paused to fire a wild burst at them, which splintered the windscreen of the first one and sent it careering off the road to overturn in the ditch, scattering screaming Dutch soldiers everywhere, and then he was running straight for them: David against Goliath.

The second truck screamed to a halt. The driver of the third did not react so quickly. He smashed his truck into the second one and for a moment there was complete confusion as Dutch soldiers dropped into the muddy ditches or milled around while red-faced NCOs blew their whistles and officers bellowed orders and counter-orders.

Otto pelted forward, zig-zagging like a centre-forward as the first wild bullets started to cut the air around him, firing as he ran, knowing instinctively, although he had never been in action before, that boldness was the key to success on a battlefield.

A Dutchman popped up out of the ditch, fired and popped down again. Otto continued running. The Dutchman popped up again. This time Otto was waiting for him. The savage burst ripped his face into a red oozing pulp, his features sliding down it like molten candle wax. He fell back.

Otto slipped on the mud and fell feet-first into the ditch. Everywhere the confused, completely demoralised Dutch infantry started throwing away their rifles, raising their hands and crying '*Kamerad . . . nicht schiessen, Kamerad!*'

'You're no fucking comrades of mine!' Otto cried angrily and smashed the nearest one across the head with the butt of his Schmeisser. 'Get running back to that bridge and surrender!' He pressed the trigger of his mp and the mud was churned up into crazy little spouts at their feet.

Wildly, hopping around in a crazy polka, the ashen-faced Dutch infantry fled from the ditch and streamed across the field to where the Count's positions were, hands above their heads, screaming their little litany. '*Kamerad . . . nicht schiessen . . . Kamerad, bitte nicht schiessen!*'

Otto dived into the cab of the first truck. The driver lay moaning across the wheel, his face full of glass splinters so that he gleamed as if with ice.

Otto heaved with his shoulder and the man slammed out of the hanging door and dropped to the ground with more of a sigh than a moan now, as if life were simply too much. To his immediate front, Otto could see tiny figures running for cover on the ridge-line, and then in the foreground a handful of soldiers, grouped around a portly officer carrying what seemed a wreath.

He didn't wait to find out what their intentions were. Instead he gave them a quick burst, swinging his mp from side to side with some difficulty in the tight confines of the cab. A couple of them whirled around and slammed to the ground like broken dolls whilst the rest shot up their hands like children at school, anxious to be excused.

Otto dropped out of the cab, his lethal instinct and energy beginning to drain from him rapidly now, and approached them suspiciously, machine-pistol at the ready.

But all fight had gone from the Dutch infantry and Otto could see that he'd get no trouble from them, an impression that was confirmed an instant later when the elderly officer with what looked like a wreath in his hand said in German, 'We surrender.'

'I thought you would,' Otto said, noting that on the ridge beyond the infantry were dropping to the ground, as if they were going to make a more determined fight of it than the men of the 26th Regiment had. 'What's that you've got in your hand?' he asked.

The Dutch officer turned it round so that Otto could see it more clearly. It was a silver painted wreath with the figure 'thirty' in the centre, also in silver. 'I was going to celebrate my thirtieth anniversary of joining the 26th today when you appeared so unexpectedly,' the portly officer replied. 'Never fired a shot in anger before, not even at the niggers out in the Dutch Indies, and now I go and lose my first battle on my anniversary of all days!'

For a moment Otto thought the Dutchman was going to break down and cry. 'Never mind,' he consoled the crestfallen man, 'you'll have something to talk about with your cronies, now that you've retired.'

'*Retired?* . . . Oh, yes, I see what you mean. I don't suppose you Germans will be wanting to keep the Dutch Army intact.' His fat face creased in a suddenly worried frown. 'I wonder what will happen to my pension?' He looked directly at Otto. 'Would you happen to know what provision your authorities have made on that score?'

Otto shook his head in mock wonder. It seemed the Royal Netherlands Army had its share of crazy men too. 'Let's not worry about your pension, pal,' he snapped with some irritation. 'Those blokes up there on the ridge, are you listening to me?' The Dutchman shook himself out of his reverie, 'Yes, I'm listening.'

'Well, they're about to open fire in a minute. Let's have them out of those holes with their hands up.'

The Dutchman shook his head so strongly that his fat jowls wobbled. 'Impossible,' he said.

'What do you mean – *impossible*?'

'They're the Queen's Grenadiers. They *never* surrender!'

'How do you shitting well know?' Otto cried in exasperation, knowing that if he didn't act soon, the Dutch on the ridge would open fire. 'You cheeseheads haven't fought a war for over a hundred years. So let's have a go and see what happens.'

The Dutchman's shoulders slumped in defeat. 'All right,' he said miserably, handing his precious wreath to one of the infantrymen, 'but let me assure you that I'm doing this under strong protest.'

'Protest all you want. Come on.'

Deliberately the two of them left the others and stumped across the damp field towards the Queen's Grenadiers on the ridge, the Dutchman pausing every couple of moments to cup his hands around his mouth and cry in Dutch, '*Vriend!*'

Finally when they were about two hundred metres away from the Grenadiers' positions, Otto halted and said to the Dutchman, 'All right, you go on alone, but remember I've got this,' he slapped the mp, 'pointing right at yer fat arse.'

'I'll remember,' the Dutchman said nervously, 'and what am I supposed to say?'

'Tell them,' Otto improvised hastily, remembering

the dialogue of the Wild West films of his youth when the outlaws had been trapped by the posse, 'that they haven't got a chance. Their only hope is to surrender.'

'But they're the Gren—'

'Go on,' Otto gave him a rude shove in the back and the Dutchman stumbled forward, looking very unhappy, crying the word 'friend' like a medieval leper tinkling his bell to advise his presence. When he was a hundred metres away, a tall scowling Dutch officer, who seemed to be carrying a sword just like the Count, sprang dramatically onto the ridge and shouted something in Dutch.

The fat officer stopped, as if he had been shot.

There was a moment's interchange of question and counter-question and then the man on the ridge with the sword shook his head and roared in German, obviously for Otto's benefit, 'Never . . . The Queen's Grenadiers never surrender!'

'Oh shit,' Otto said and gave up. 'Come on, cheesehead, let's get back to the bridge.

The fat Dutchman needed no urging. Hurriedly he turned and started running heavily towards a waiting Otto. It was then that the man on the ridge drew his pistol and taking very careful aim, pulled the trigger.'

'Why you rotten treacherous shit—'

The crack of the pistol drowned the rest of Otto's angry outburst.

The fat Dutchman howled with pain and staggered a few paces more to collapse in Otto's arms, a great scarlet flower growing by the second between his shoulders. 'It's been a funny anniversary,' he gasped and then he was dead.

THREE

'Counter-attack,' the Count said through parched lips and wiped the beads of sweat delicately from his dirty forehead.

Now it was midday and the May sun was hot. Most of the Brandenburgers, digging ever deeper holes around the bridge, had stripped to the waist and there was a relay of men down to the water to fill their water-bottles in spite of the fact that a dead Dutch soldier floated on its stagnant surface.

'What do you mean – counter-attack?' Otto said irritably. He was angry with himself, the Count, the cheeseheads, the whole war. It was six hours now since they had spotted the German armoured spearheads crawling up the roads towards the bridge and he had felt his ordeal was over at last; they would be relieved soon. But that wasn't to be. Just as the lead tank had commenced its drive up the bridge road, there had been a cry of warning from the air-lookout and four Dutch Fokkers fighters had dropped out of the morning air, their machine-guns blazing. Tracer had started to howl off the Mark III's armour like ping-pong balls. But the tank driver had panicked. As the Fokkers had come howling in once more at tree-top height, mgs chattering furiously, he had swung his tank round and smashed head-on into the tank behind. In a flash the road had been blocked and with the armoured column's petrol-bowsers suddenly burning furiously, the great drive had come to an abrupt halt, with badly scared and wounded tankers hobbling for cover everywhere. Now it seemed that they wouldn't be relieved until after dark.

'Of course,' the Count snapped, still playing the role of leader-of-men. It's military SOP – standard-operating-procedure, you know,' he added by way of explanation. 'That's what we old front-officers call it.' He laughed lightly.

Otto groaned. Even now the lunatics of the *Abwehr* couldn't face up to the reality of the battlefield and sudden death. God knows how Gertie, Maps, Brass Eggs and all the rest of the spy-school cretins were getting on in their allotted sectors!

'Out there,' the Count indicated the smoke-shrouded positions of the Queen's Grenadiers, 'they're probably assembling their forces at this very moment. First there'll be the Fokkers.'

'Yes,' Otto agreed dourly. 'The Fokkers!'

'Then the artillery bombardment to soften us up.'

'We're soft enough in this mob already.'

The Count didn't seem to hear. 'After that, there'll be the tanks and finally when they judge we're ripe for the killing—' Otto winced at the word, but said nothing. '– they'll put in their infantry. The jolly old bayonet attack,' the Count said happily. 'Cold steel and all that.' He made a ripping sound, and Otto shuddered. 'Now what are we going to do about it, eh?'

'Surrender perhaps,' Otto suggested cautiously.

'Nonsense, Otto!' the Count snorted. 'Shot and shell can't do much harm to old soldiers like our brave chaps.' He indicated the dusky 'South African' who was busy digging into the side of his trench, looking for worms again. 'See how they're burrowing ever deeper like the veterans they are, Otto. No, my boy, once the hate is over, we'll strike!'

'What do you mean?' Otto asked in spite of himself.

'Catch them off guard!' The Count smashed a fist into the palm of his left hand. 'Hit them in the flank before they know what's hit them!' He laughed jovially, the complete mercenary now. 'Catch them with their knickers down, what, Otto?'

'The only person I'd like to catch with knickers down is that blonde I was snaking back in Duren,' Otto said mournfully.

'There'll be plenty of time for that sort of thing later, Otto. There'll be wine and women enough for my heroes, once this bloody business is over.' He looked hard at Otto. 'I know I'm asking a great deal, Otto. You've already done your share – and more. Never fear, there'll be a medal in it for you.' He cleared his throat, as if he were suddenly overcome with emotion, and Otto could have sworn there was a glint of tears in his eyes at that moment. 'Otto, I am asking you to lead that flank attack.'

Surprisingly enough Otto heard himself saying, as if someone else were using his voice, 'Oh, all right, give up, I'll go!' Five minutes later at the head of ten Brandenburgers, heavily laden with weapons and ammunition so that they plodded through the ploughed field to their front like weary farmhands, they were on their way, encouraged by the Count calling, 'And remember, there'll be a medal in this for you, Otto – a very good one.'

'Send it to my shitting next-of-kin!' Otto told himself sourly, but to the Count he said nothing. He couldn't, for his heart was too heavy with the realisation that he had been conned again.

Five minutes later the little patrol disappeared into the firs to the right of the bridgehead.

'I can hear men moving,' the dusky 'South African' hissed, raising his head from the ground.

'Christ, and they talk about the white man's burden!' Otto groaned and wiped the sweat from his forehead, his nostrils full of the heavy cloying scent of resin. 'I can't hear a shitting thing.'

The dusky 'South African' shrugged easily and taking

a worm out of his pocket, said, 'My iron ration' by way of explanation. He began to chew contentedly on the disgusting thing, as if he had done his duty and there were nothing more to be said or done.

Otto bit his bottom lip, face set in a worried frown. They had been hidden in the trees on the right flank for two hours now and none of the moves that the Count had predicted the Dutch would make had occurred. There had been no fighter attack or artillery bombardment. Indeed the only noise was that of the bees buzzing around and the steady drip-drip of resin escaping from the trees. One could have thought the Dutch had decided to discontinue the war and had gone home to their fat cheesehead wives and those raw herrings they ate all the time.

'What are we going to do – if he's right?' another of the 'South Africans' asked, indicating the dusky one busy with his worm. 'Those Kaffirs know things we don't know. Besides they are half-animals as it is. They can see and hear as good as a springbok.'

'Better,' the dusky one said, raising his head momentarily, in no way offended that he had been called a 'Kaffir'. 'They're out there all right. And they're not *konijn*.'

'What?'

'Rabbit,' the other 'South African' translated the Afrikaans word for him.

'All right,' Otto made his decision. 'I'm gonna have a look. You lot of foreigners follow at fifty metres. Do as I do. And if I beat it, you do too. Cos in the mood I'm in at the moment, I'm not going to be sending out special invitations. And you,' he hissed at the dusky one. 'Swallow that sodding worm! Quick! It's giving me the shitting creeps!'

Obediently the dusky 'South African' pursed his lips and sucked hard like an Italian swallowing spaghetti. The worm, its russet-brown tail still wagging valiantly, disappeared suddenly.

Otto shuddered.

'All right, *baas*?' the dusky one said and belched pleasurably.

Otto shook his head and started to creep forward through the firs, machine-pistol at the ready, while the others followed, treading carefully, their weapons cocked. Otto said a quick prayer to heaven that there were no itchy trigger-fingers among them.

Time passed leadenly as the little group stole through the trees, placing their feet down with exaggerated caution, as if they were walking across eggs. Now Otto could hear the faint buzz of voices to their front. The worm-eater had been right. There were men out there – and they could only be Dutch. He held up his hand to indicate the others should halt. Slowly, very slowly, he crept forward, a nerve beginning to tic uncontrollably at his left temple, the hand holding his Schmeisser abruptly wet with sweat; and he knew why. He was scared, shit scared. *Christ*, a little voice at the back of his head said, *why don't you fuck off, while there's still time? Go on, pick your legs up under your arms. A bloke can get killed dead out here!*

But Otto, at least the Otto moving so purposefully through the hot trees, did not seem to hear. He continued his cautious progress in the direction from which the voices came.

All right, the little voice sneered, *be a shitting hero – and see what it gets you!*

Next instant Otto had parted the sticky fir fronds and was staring at the half-dozen fat Dutchmen, their faces red with the heat, tunics open as they sprawled in the grass in front of the two small tanks, bottles of beer clutched in their hands, half-eaten tins of meat with spoons sticking out of them scattered before them in the grass, looking for all the world like a bunch of picnickers.

'Standard-Operating-Procedure!' Otto whispered scornfully to himself, remembering the Count's words. So this was the great counter-attack: a bunch of half-pissed cheeseheads dodging the column in a nice quiet hideaway in the forest. He laughed bitterly. There was going to be no battle this particular afternoon. Slowly and carefully he began to close the bushes, prior to crawling away and leaving the cheeseheads to their beer. It was too hot to play soldier any more. But that wasn't to be.

Across at the second little tank, the radio began to crackle suddenly.

'*Groote Gott!*' one of the Dutchmen with stars on his shoulders cursed. He stumbled to his feet and stalked over to the tank with the air of a man sorely tried on a hot day like this.

Otto hesitated. What was going on?

The NCO swung himself onto the turret of the tank and grabbing the earphones from within, slipped them over his shaven skull, while the others waited expectantly, some of them even forgetting to drink their beer.

Even though he did not understand a word of Dutch and was anyway unable to hear the message coming through that radio, Otto knew that authority was speaking – he could see it by the way the NCO's face hardened and his shoulders straightened – and the orders that were winging their way along the airwaves were not to the NCO's liking.

In the end the NCO saluted and dropped from the turret, pulling off the earphones with an angry gesture. Otto's heart sank. He knew before the NCO spoke what his orders were: mount up and start the engines.

Slowly, as if in a trance, Otto raised his Schmeisser and aimed at the centre of the NCO's well-filled tunic while he rapped out angry orders to his red-faced soldiers, now beginning to move to their feet reluctantly, but obediently.

He pressed the trigger. The Schmeisser screamed into high-pitched, hysterical life, sending the birds screaming from the trees.

The NCO looked down at the sudden line of red-flecked button holes stitched across the front of his tunic stupidly, then he gave a little leap and slammed against the side of the tank, his head lolling to one side, tongue hanging out of it, to remain standing thus like some village idiot overcome by the heat.

In an instant all was chaos and confusion.

The Dutch soldiers burst apart, running in all directions, Otto's machine-pistol speeding them on their way, his bullets thrashing the foliage like heavy summer rain, while the Brandenburgers burst out of the trees, firing from the hip as they came, whooping hilariously at the fleeing enemy until in the end, Otto cried with all his strength, 'For Chrissake, let 'em go . . . *let them run! The way they've been stuffing their fat cheesehead guts, they'll have a heart attack anyway . . . Save your slugs!*'

The Brandenburgers' fire died away and then there was no noise at all, save the awed intake of their breath as they eyed their booty, intoning, 'We've captured their armour . . . Two tanks! Now what do you say to that?' Here and there the 'South Africans' shook hands triumphantly.

'Oh, knock it off, will you?' Otto said finally in disgust. 'What good are tanks to us? Unless one of you geniuses can drive one of the tin cans?'

'I know how to drive a tractor,' the 'South African' who had called the dusky one a 'Kaffir' volunteered.

Otto ignored him and walked slowly around the two abandoned vehicles, eyeing them curiously. It would be quite a triumph if they could manage to get them back to the bridgehead. It would convince the Count that he had done his duty to the best of his ability. Besides, their armour would provide ideal protection in case the Dutch fighter-planes returned.

'Good to have if the Fokkers come back,' he said thoughtfully.

'Yes, the Fokkers,' they agreed in unison.

'Let me have a go,' the dusky 'South African' said. 'I think I can get it started.'

'What does a mealy Kaffir like you know about motors?' the other one said scornfully. 'Hell, the first time you wore britches was when you came to Germany!'

'Your mother gets fucked by Cape baboons,' the dusky one said mildly.

'Why you black bastard—'

Hastily Otto intervened between the two 'South Africans'. 'All right, all right. Start your own war in your own free time,' he said. 'Officially, remember, we're fighting the cheeseheads.' He turned to the dusky one. 'Go on then, if you think you can do it.'

'Yes *baas*.'

He disappeared inside and Otto waited tensely with the others, telling himself that the Dutch who had fled might well have contacted the main body of their troops by now, while he fumbled with the wheels and levers within the captured tank.

Suddenly the tank's engine began to whine like an asthmatic in extremis. Thick blue diesel smoke started to flood out of its exhaust. It coughed a couple of times and then the motor burst into ear-splitting noise. A lurch and it started to creak backwards.

Hurriedly the spectators scattered out of its path, all save the contemptuous 'South African'. The track passed right over his foot and stalled, leaving him trapped there, his eyes rolling, screaming frantically, 'Get it off . . . get if off, for Chrissake!'

Happily the dusky one popped his head out of the turret, apparently not seeing his trapped, screaming comrade, and said, 'It's very easy to control. There are just two handles. The one brakes the right track, the other the left. That's the way you turn. Push them both straight ahead—'

'Just move it a bit, will you?' Otto interrupted his explanation. 'This chap here,' he indicated the trapped 'South African' whose face had turned crimson and who was making little strangled noises, jerking his head from side to side as if he were choking, 'seems to be having some trouble.'

'Oh him,' the dusky one said, as if noticing the man

for the first time. 'Hang on!'

He disappeared inside, started the motor once more and creaked forward a few paces, freeing the trapped man.

'Thank God,' he cried, hopping around on one foot, hugging the other tenderly. 'I swear that black nigger would have had the flipper off'n me in another minute! Wait till I'm—'

The thick crump of a heavy cannon close behind drowned the rest of his threat. With a tremendous roar like that of an express train howling through a tunnel at high speed, the first shell tore the afternoon stillness apart frighteningly.

'Holy strawsack!' Otto yelled. '*The cheeseheads!*'

Led by a tank, a group of cautious Dutch infantry, bodies bent as if against heavy rain, was advancing towards them some five hundred metres away, with to their right the same officer who had shot the fat Dutchman waving his sword at them in encouragement.

The 'South Africans' panicked. 'What are we going to do?' someone screamed in terror, while others started to throw down their weapons. 'Run like hell!' Otto cried above the thunder of the enemy tank's gun. He ducked hastily as a shell exploded fifty metres away, showering his helmet with soil and gravel and opening up a great steaming brown pit that looked like the work of a gigantic mole. 'Come on, get that tank moving!' The dusky one dropped inside. Madly the 'South Africans' scrambled onto the deck, crouching down behind the protection of the turret.

Next to them the other tank reeled like a ship at sea struck by a sudden hurricane. An instant later it exploded in a blinding flash of violent flame. Tracer ammunition began crazily zig-zagging upwards into the burning sky and what looked like a football sailed by Otto's ducked head and disappeared into the bushes. In passing he recognised it as that of the man whose foot had been trapped. 'Some people always have either their feet or their heads in the shit,' he commented, then he was scuttling for cover inside the turret while below the rattled worm-eater fumbled with frantic fingers, trying to get the tank started again.

His belt caught on a lever. Cursing and sweating with fearful rage, he tugged himself free. Next moment the gun at his side exploded. The breech slid back and a gleaming brass shell-case tumbled to the floor.

Coughing and spluttering in the acrid smoke which had flooded the compartment from the open breech, Otto peered through the little periscope and gasped with shock. To his front the Dutch tank was burning furiously, while the infantry milled around, splashing its steel sides with the contents of their water-bottles, while the big ugly officer waved his sword at them in impotent fury.

'You'd do better to piss on it,' Otto said, much cheered up by the sight.

Then with a roar the motor started once more and below the dusky 'South African' had smashed home reverse and they were tearing through the forest at a tremendous speed, snapping over the firs as if they were made of matchwood.

'The Battle of the Gennep Bridgehead!', as the Goebells press would herald it in the morning was over, and unknowingly Otto was a hero – for a while, at least.

FOUR

'What do you think?' the dusky 'South African' whispered, a little anxiously.

'I've given up thinking for the day, I'm that buggered,' Otto whispered back and stared up at the blacked-out structure which had appeared so surprisingly and suddenly out of nowhere, in the middle of the fir forest. For hours now they had been blundering through the thick firs, long after the sound of the guns had died away behind them, trying to work their way back to the bridgehead, and becoming increasingly lost in the process.

Now it was completely dark with a half-moon casting a faint silver light over the scene to their front and silent, save for the heavy ticking of the tank's diesels.

'I'm hungry,' the 'South African' said plaintively. 'Haven't had a bite to eat for hours . . . I could really go a big fat juicy worm at this minute.'

Otto said nothing. Instead he stared at the turetted structure to his front. The place looked like something out of a peacetime UFA horror movie: a gothic monster of dark battlements and towers, silent and somehow menacing in the ghostly silvery light. It made Otto think of vampires and werewolves and corpses called back from the dead. He shuddered.

'We've only got diesel for another couple of kilometres,' the dusky 'South African' said grumpily.

Still Otto said nothing as he eyed the place and considered what to do next.

They must be kilometres away from the fighting by now, he told himself and reasoned that the lonely gothic castle, set out here in the forest, could hardly be of any importance. What was there to defend here? His stomach rumbled noisely and abruptly he remembered he had not eaten since the previous day. Suddenly he was ravenously hungry.

'Listen,' he said urgently, turning to the men crouched behind the tank, staring at the silent castle, 'we'll have a go. You,' he nodded to one of the 'South Africans'. 'Shin up that pole over there and cut the telephone wires. We don't want them calling for help to the outside world.'

Obediently the man started to climb the pole.

'The rest of you,' Otto ordered. 'Follow me. No shooting. I've resigned from the Army for this day. All we want is to nick some grub, see if the cheeseheads have got some diesel for the tin can, and then we're off again back to the bridge. By this time, the Army stubble-hoppers should have linked up with the Count. Clear?'

'Clear,' his men echoed as one.

'Good, let's go!'

On the tips of their toes, strung out in single file, hugging the shadows, hardly daring to breathe, the little group of soldiers worked their way by the tangled branches of small ornamental trees that lined the entrance to the strange place, throwing fearful glances at the gothic battlements, outlined a stark, menacing black by the cloudrack.

Time and time again Otto tried to convince himself that it was just his imagination and there was no one behind them, but he didn't succeed; and once again he would fling a nervous glance over his shoulder, heart beating like a trip-hammer, only to find that there was, indeed, no one there.

Slowly they progressed down the long *allée*, Otto's fertile imagination peopling the ominous shadows with phantom shapes, until they were halted by what appeared to be a blank wall, overgrown with ivy, in which insects rustled frighteningly.

'What now?' someone croaked hoarsely.

The dusky 'South African' touched Otto on the shoulder.

He started, the bile of panic welling up sickeningly in his throat. 'What is it?' he asked thickly.

The dusky 'South African' swallowed the spider he had just found in the ivy and whispered. 'There's a door over there, *Sonderfuhrer*.'

Otto followed the direction of his outstretched hand and saw the faint line of yellow light escaping from underneath what he now saw clearly was a door. For a moment, however, he was rooted to the spot, not knowing what to do until the 'South African' said, his mouth full of another spider, 'Well, why don't you knock on it?'

'But we're the invaders,' Otto protested, finding his voice at last. 'I mean invaders don't just knock at doors like salesmen!'

The other man shrugged. 'It's up to you, *Sonderfuhrer*. Just walk in, if you like.'

Otto swallowed hard and summoning up the last of his courage, he tiptoed to the door and fumbled for the knob. He found it at the very moment when, to his horror, it started to turn in his hand. He stumbled back, as if the big iron handle had been red-hot.

Slowly the great oaken door creaked open, the hinges squeaking rustily, and yellow light flooded into the *allée*, illuminating the scared, ashen faces of the soldiers crouched there, nervously clutching their weapons.

A tall skinny old man stood there, dressed in black, looking down the length of his great beak of a nose, as if he had just discovered an unpleasant odour and was trying to ascertain its exact source. 'We heard your vehicle approach, sir,' he addressed Otto in excellent if somewhat funereal-sounding German. 'I hope you didn't have any difficulty finding a parking place?'

'No . . . not at all,' Otto stuttered.

'Good sir. Now if you will follow me, sir.'

Dumbstruck Otto crossed the threshold while the Dutchman held back the door. Slowly the first of the 'South Africans' began to follow, but the Dutchman barred his entrance with a politely but firmly raised hand. 'Tradesmen's entrance to the rear, soldier.' With a solemn creak like the lid of a tomb being lowered for the last time, the door closed behind Otto and he was cut off from his men in the long gloomy corridor, its grey stone walls hung with the fading portraits of bearded nineteenth century worthies who stared down at the dirty, ragged soldier with heavy disdain.

'This way, sir,' said the man – later Otto found out he was indeed the castle's butler – 'if you would be so kind?'

With due ceremony the butler strode down the long grey corridor and into another and another, their boots echoing hollowly until finally he paused in front of a large carved wooden door to tap on it delicately with his knuckles before throwing it open with a flourish and saying, '*Bitte, Herr Leutnant, treten Sie näher.*'

Otto 'approached nearer' and stopped abruptly.

A really beautiful woman stood there in front of the crackling wood fire in the great hearth. She couldn't have been more than twenty, but she had that cold northern loveliness that made her appear much older, with a long fine face that appeared to have been carved from marble.

'You are in charge, Lieutenant?' she said in good German, giving the dirty, ragged young man a haughty look.

'Yes, I suppose I am.'

She advanced to him, back erect, small but well-formed breasts thrusting at the thin silk of her blouse like noses trying to get out. 'I will not give you my hand,' she announced stopping a metre away from him. 'After all you are my enemy. But my name is van Elst, *Countess van Elst.*'

A little confused Otto stuttered something.

'If you assure me on your word as an officer and a gentleman not to hurt my people,' she continued, 'I will give you my promise that I shall not attempt to escape or in any way try to sabotage your installations here.'

Numbly Otto heard himself doing just that – as an officer and gentleman.

She gave him a cold little smile, revealing perfect, pearl-white, little teeth. 'Good, then that is settled.' She nodded to the waiting butler. '*Dank u, Mulder . . . De kamer met een bed.*'

The butler gave a stiff little bow, a look of disapproval on his face, and disappeared noiselessly.

Otto frowned. Had she said something about a bed?

But he had no time to consider that question, for the beautiful young countess said with the same frosty smile as before. 'Of course, you will wish to dine with me? My people will take care of your soldiers. Follow me and I will show you where you can . . . er,' she blushed suddenly, 'wash your hands.'

In a trance, Otto followed.

They dined in candlelight. Elderly servants, male and female, clad in rusty black who seemed to creak as they crept in bearing silver dish after dish of food, served them in absolute silence under the watchful and still disapproving gaze of Mulder, the butler. Otto ate greedily. He had never tasted food like this in all his life. Wine flowed freely too, red, white, sweet, dry; there were even bottles of French champagne, a drink Otto was now tasting for the first time, though in years to come it would become his favourite tipple.

By the time the servants had deposited the *mokka* and decanters of assorted strong Dutch cordials and disappeared together with the butler, Otto was in a very happy state indeed and in the flickering candlelight seemed to be having some difficulty in seeing the beautiful, if cold countess correctly, so that every now and again he had to close one eye in order to focus on her.

Whether it was the influence of wine on him or not, it seemed to Otto that the Dutch aristocrat's behaviour had changed somewhat too, as if she were beginning to thaw at last. Somehow or other her white-blonde hair had come loose and cascaded over her naked shoulders and she appeared to lean towards him a great deal across the table to reveal the tops of those delightful little breasts. Once indeed, he could have sworn he saw two pink-red cherries which were her nipples.

'I am betrothed naturally,' he remembered her saying once afterwards.

She indicated a large photograph on the marble mantelpiece above the crackling logs. Otto caught a blurred look of a scarfaced, surly young man in uniform who, surprisingly enough, seemed vaguely familiar. 'Dirk van Dongeren.'

'Has he got a big dong?' he asked drunkenly.

Aristocrat that she was, she had ignored the impolite question, and said. 'Undoubtedly he will be serving with his regiment – the Grenadiers – at the front at this very minute. But I am sure that he'll understand that I couldn't help it.' She gave a great sigh.

'Understand what?'

But again she had not appeared to hear his question.

Then events grew very confused, especially after she insisted that he could drink a good strong Dutch *genever* with her. 'Made by Fokkin and Fokkin of Schiedamn, the best,' she declared stoutly.

'Fokkers – and now Fokkin and Fokkin,' Otto had slurred, shaking his head and trying to clear away the mist that threatened to enshroud him. 'Funny country . . . very funny indeed.'

Time passed. Somewhere an old clock chimed midnight with grave inexorability. In the hearth the logs had turned to glowing red embers. The castle creaked at regular intervals, and outside the trees sighed in the wind.

Countess van Elst, crouched in front of the fire on the

thick white rug and – apparently accidentally – revealed a great deal of delightful white thigh above her sheer black silk stocking. She gave a great sigh, breaking the heavy drunken silence. 'I am very sure he'll understand.' She stretched up to look at the photo of her fiancé with sad eyes to reveal even more of her delightful white thigh.

'Understand what?' Otto mumbled thickly, waking up out of a drunken sleep suddenly.

'That I have been forced to sacrifice my honour,' she answered simply, gaze demure, hands folded, as if in resignation, across her silken lap. 'I know you and your countrymen. If I do not give myself,' she lowered her eyes for a moment in embarrassment, '*voluntarily*, you will undoubtedly rip the clothes from me, bit by bit. First my blouse, then my skirt, then—'

'Stop!' Otto said wildly. 'I have no intention of—'

'And finally it will be . . . *my underthings* so that I am completely naked and my poor little woman's body will be yours to do with what you wish,' she continued, speaking more hurriedly now, as if she could not complete this dreadful litany quickly enough. 'To slake your brutal perverted desires on – *all night*!'

'But . . . but . . .' Otto stuttered, absolutely confused now. But already, Countess van Elst was beginning to blow out the candles for the night . . .

FIVE

'You must realise, *mein Herr*,' the countess said firmly, as she stood in front of a drunkenly swaying Otto in the cold moonlight, 'that I am doing this thing under duress.'

Otto made a lunge at her, but she avoided him easily. 'At this moment of my country's greatest need,' she continued, 'I have neither the time nor the interest for sexual matters. They are nothing to me now while my Homeland fights for its survival, absolutely nothing. You will have your cruel way with me . . . but without my aid.' She hooked her thumbs inside his flies, which he had been fumbling with drunkenly and in vain, and ripped downwards as if she were peeling the skin off a banana.

'Oh Christ!' Otto gasped at what was revealed and with the shock of it fell over backwards onto the big single bed, trousers around his ankles, legs stuck in the air.

She sighed, as if sorely tried. 'What monsters you Germans are. How your women must suffer!' Slightly roughly she pulled the trousers and then his shoes off, saying sternly. 'The shirt, you do yourself. It's neither healthy nor hygienic to sleep in the clothes you wear during the day.'

Completely confused and befuddled now, Otto struggled to get the shirt over his head and when he had done so, he found her lying on the far side of the bed, as stiff as a corpse, a cold proud beauty, giving off an aura of icy aristocratic disdain. But now Otto was so full of booze and lewdness that he cared neither for her stand-offishness nor her little games. He rolled towards her. She shrieked and screwed her eyes tightly closed and let it happen, as stiff as a board so that he might well have been screwing a corpse.

But much later, he awoke to feel her tiny hand creeping purposefully across his thigh and then onto his stomach and her warm, excited breathing close to his right ear and he knew that Countess van Elst might appear to be all chaste purity, as cold as ice, but underneath she was as randy as a baboon!

Afterwards he went to sleep, telling himself that war wasn't too bad a business after all; one certainly got to know a better class of individual during it.

The shock of the first mortar shell exploding against the castle-wall threw Otto out of bed. 'What the hell was that?' he gasped.

In the bed, the countess pulled the sheet up modestly over her naked breasts, while outside there sounded what appeared to be hunting bugles.

Now it was her turn to gasp. 'It's the . . . Queen's Grenadiers!' she shrieked. 'It's my betrothed come to rescue me!'

'You mean the Dong?' Otto asked from the floor.

She nodded numbly, as the wall trembled with the impact of another mortar bomb exploding against it.

'Oh shit!' Otto said. 'I must say your fiancé has a funny way of showing his concern. He could kill you dead with one of those shitting things.' He ducked hastily as the leaded window blew out, showering him with glass.

'He's very impetuous,' she agreed. 'Act first and think afterwards. But then,' she added, as if that explained everything, 'he is an officer.' On his hands and knees, yelping with pain as the glass dug into his palms, Otto crawled naked to the shattered window, while the countess watched him with sudden interest, all thoughts of Baron Dirk van Dongeren forgotten again because of what she saw.

Cautiously he peeped out.

Down below small green-clad soldiers were doubling to left and right, their weapons at the ready, while the officer with the sword directed the fire of a small mortar, located in a clump of bushes at the end of the *allée*, his blade flashing silver in the moonlight as he brought it down each time as a signal for the sweating crew to fire.

Otto sucked his teeth in dismay. In a minute or two the cheeseheads would have the castle completely surrounded and they would be cut off. *Yes, and that won't be the only thing that might be cut off!* that cynical little voice at the back of his head said maliciously. Otto shuddered. 'Of course, it wouldn't look too good if that Dong bloke found him in bed with his fiancée, and he had seen enough of war already to know that soldiers were inclined to hasty, violent decisions on the field of battle. What had she just said? Act first and think afterwards. Instinctively his hand grabbed his genitals protectively. He had to get away before it was too late!

He crawled back to the bed. 'Get dressed!' he hissed, madly looking for his own clothes strewn on the floor.

'Not while you're watching me,' she protested, 'running your lecherous gaze over my naked body. My breasts, my stomach, my—'

'Oh for Chrissake, don't start that business again!' Otto moaned, flinging himself into his uniform, as the castle trembled under the impact of yet another explosion and from down below, he could hear the first quavering cries of surrender from the 'South Africans'.

He tumbled into his boots and slung the Schmeisser over his shoulder. The countess still lay in bed, the sheet pulled tightly across her breasts, displaying her nipples prettily. But Otto was too frightened of what the Dong would do if he found them together in the bedroom like this to be interested in the countess's nipples. 'I'm off. I'll try to do a bunk before they get into the castle.'

She nodded her approval. 'I can see that you are an officer and a gentleman after all, trying to protect my reputation in this way.'

'No, I'm just shitting scared stiff!' Otto snorted and with that statement he was gone.

The countess lay back smiling and put her tiny hand between her legs. It had been a very pleasant night. Just like that fool Dirk to spoil her little bit of fun. She gave a sigh of pleasure. Still she might as well stroke the cat until he came blundering in in his usual clumsy manner. She closed her eyes and concentrated on the task in hand.

On tiptoe, weapon at the ready, Otto stole down the long gloomy corridor. Muted by the thick stone walls, he could hear the cries in Dutch and German below and reasoned that the servants were opening the great door to let the 'South Africans' go out and surrender so that the mortar bombardment would stop. Otto sniffed. Let them get on with it, he told himself. As for himself, he suspected that it would be unwise, very unwise, to do the same. Somehow or other he had to escape. But how?

Carefully he opened the door to his front. It creaked abominably. He peered through it. The next corridor was empty too. Perhaps, he thought, he might be able to get to the ground floor and open a window. While the 'South Africans' surrendered, with a bit of luck, he could sneak away into the darkness. His mind made up, he sped down the corridor, hushing down the steps to his front, pausing every now and again in the cover of shadows to listen, holding his breath and trying to make out what was going on, while his heart thumped fearfully, as if it might burst out of his rib cage at any moment.

Once he heard a voice close by speaking in Dutch. Hurriedly he ducked behind an arras and waited trembling while the sounds had died away, before continuing.

Now he judged that he was getting very close to the ground floor. The excited babble in German and Dutch was louder too, and he could hear some sort of argument going on in which the word 'door' was repeated several times in both languages. He guessed that the 'South Africans' were having second thoughts about going outside to surrender just like that. Perhaps they, too, had realised just how trigger-happy soldiers are in action. But the obscene crack and thump of the mortar had stopped and Otto reasoned that the Dutch had decided the Germans had had enough and were ready to give in.

He quickened his pace. He needed the confusion of the surrender to get away unseen. He opened another door. Moonlight streamed in through a line of leaded window, transforming the grey gloom of the corridor beyond into a bright silver.

Otto hesitated. Anyone opening the door at the far end would see him immediately in that light. But there were the windows he needed; he had to take that chance. Hurriedly slinging his Schmeisser, he sped across it to the nearest window. With trembling fingers he found the catch and tugged. Nothing happened. The damn thing didn't move!

'*Shit!*' he cursed to himself and tried again, exerting all his strength, aware now of the great door that led into the *allée* being creaked open.

Still the window did not move. For a moment he stood there, shoulders heaving with the strain, at a loss. The catch had probably rusted into the fitting. He needed something to force it.

Talking to himself, he fumbled around on the window-sill, searching around for something to smash against the handle; and then he had it. The iron butt of the Schmeisser! Hastily he unslung it and turned the machine-pistol round. He counted three and slammed the butt against the catch.

The noise seemed tremendous. It echoed and re-echoed down the empty corridor like a roll of thunder. Otto froze. The noise was fit to wake the dead.

But down below the door continued to open and he could hear confused shouting in Dutch. The infantry were coming in to take the Germans' surrender. He hadn't been heard obviously.

Reassured, he slammed the butt of his machine-pistol against the catch once more, and again, praying to himself that he wouldn't be heard, belabouring it with all his strength.

Now the catch started to move. Frantically he banged away at it, sweating now, swearing at the damn thing for not moving more quickly, the sound of heavy boots below getting louder by the second.

Suddenly it gave. Gasping, he pulled the window open. Down below there was the silver gleam of the stagnant moat, perhaps some fifteen metres away. The drop was considerable, but the water would break his fall. He clambered up onto the ledge and stared down at the water. It seemed a devil of a long way down now. Perhaps if he crouched, it wouldn't look so frightening. He knelt and prepared to jump.

But that wasn't to be. At the end of the corridor the door was flung open. Yellow light streamed into the passage. Otto swung round. A man was poised there, sword in hand, and he didn't need to be told who it was.

'Dirk van Dongeren!' the Dutch officer announced, a vulpine smile on his scarred face, as he raised his sword in mocking salute. 'You are not leaving us, sir, I trust?'

Otto flung a glance at the water below, thought better of it and, whipping off the Schmeisser, pressed the trigger. Nothing happened. The shitting thing had jammed! Probably the hammering against the catch had done it no good. Suddenly overcome by rage, he threw the mp at the grinning Dutchman, losing his balance as he did so and falling heavily to the stone-flagged floor.

Easily van Dongeren dodged the missile and strode down the corridor imperiously until he towered above the fallen Otto. Politely he held out his hand. In too much of a daze to react otherwise, Otto allowed himself to be hauled to his feet, and stood there swaying a little groggily.

The Dutchman stepped back a few paces, not taking his eyes off Otto for an instant. 'So, my German friend, you are out of luck, as we have been all this long black day. Perhaps now, the Queen's Grenadiers will strike lucky once again.' He raised his sword in salute once more and added, 'You have had your choice of weapon. Now, I think in all fairness, it is my turn.'

'What do you mean?' Otto asked dumbly.

By way of an answer, the Dutchman groped with his free hand on the wall until his fingers came in contact with the heavy nineteenth century sabre which hung there. With a grunt he tossed it to Otto, who in order to avoid being struck by it, caught it instinctively.

The Dutchman gave him that scar-faced vulpine smile of his. 'Ah, ah, I see you are an officer of the old school. It gives me pleasure. All these mechanical horses and popguns have made a mockery of warfare, don't you think? There is nothing like good old cold steel.'

'What do you mean?' Otto asked in complete bewilderment.

The Dutchman gave a little jump and landed both feet apart, big body turned sideways, crying, *'On guard, mein Herr!'*

'On guard – for what?'

His answer was the swift flash of silver and the sword missed the right side of his head by millimetres.

'Hey,' Otto cried angrily, reeling back, 'you could have shittingly well cut me with that big penknife of yours!'

'That is my aim!' van Dongeren said grimly through gritted teeth and lunged again.

'Now stop—'

Otto's protest ended in a gasp of sudden pain as the Dutchman's sword ripped through his sleeve and nicked his flesh. He darted back, holding up the heavy sabre automatically to protect his head from the blade which was slashing and cutting all about him.

'Ah,' van Dongeren smiled, 'the German style, what? Learnt on Heidelberg's *paukboden**, I'll wager. I see, I cannot underestimate you, *mein Herr*.' With renewed energy he recommenced hacking and thrusting at a terrified Otto, who staggered down the corridor under the weight of the furious attack, warding off the blows with the sabre the best he could, his whole body shaking with fear. The bastard really was going to kill him!

Now Otto started to weaken. It took a great deal of strength to keep wielding the heavy sabre from side to side, desperately parrying the Dutchman's flashing sword. In the cinema the heroes had always smiled a lot during the duel scenes, not a hair out of place, not a bead of sweat on their handsome powdered faces. Reality was a lot different. He sweated like a pig!

Van Dongeren smiled thinly, as he sensed that Otto was weakening. 'So, so,' he said like a character from a Lehar operetta, 'my German friend is beginning to feel the strain, what?'

'Oh fuck off!' Otto yelled and aimed a mighty blow with his sabre at van Dongeren's skull, which if he had connected, would have split him right down to his muddy boots.

Van Dongeren parried it easily and snarled, 'I would advise you sir, to guard your tongue. There could have been ladies present.' Their blades locked and deftly the Dutchman withdrew and, twitching his wrist, aimed quick blows to left and right of Otto's head, which Otto avoided just at the very last moment.

He fell back. Van Dongeren stumbled after him, his eyes narrowed to slits. Otto turned as if he were about to run, but he knew it would be no use. The Dutchman would not have the slightest compunction; he'd run him through the small of the back as mercilessly as some stolid Dutch burgher slicing into a salted herring.

Now the Dutchman began to lay on with all his

* Student fencing-ring.

strength, blade flashing in a silver burr. Otto reeled back. Their blades locked again. Otto held him there for a moment and tried to kick him in the crotch.

Van Dongeren dodged the kick easily. 'You must know that that sort of thing is not allowed,' he hissed angrily, eyes blazing with rage. 'It would lower the whole tone of the sport if one tolerated it.'

'*Sport!*' Otto cried. 'Christ, you're trying to shitting well kill me, you—'

His outburst ended in a cry of agony, as van Dongeren's blade sliced into his shoulder like a red-hot iron.

The intensity of that pain made him stagger back, sabre lowered, so that the Dutchman's next blow hissed by him and forced van Dongeren to stumble and almost fall.

Otto seized his advantage. With the last of his strength he threw the sabre hilt-first at the Dutchman and then he was running for his life, while behind him van Dongeren, his mouth looking as if he had smeared it with strawberry jam, spat out broken teeth and shouted thickly, 'Come back . . . come back, sir . . . We haven't finished the bout . . .'

The next instant Otto went headfirst through the open window and dived straight into the moat.

SIX

'You've cut yourself,' the dusky 'South African' whispered as they crouched there together in the bushes, watching the castle, its windows ablaze with lights now, as the Dutch soldiers ran from room to room, obviously looking for more Germans, yelling excitedly to one another as they did so.

'Yes, I nicked myself shaving,' Otto answered angrily, holding his wounded shoulder, his clothes soaked from his quick swim in the moat. 'What happened to our lot?'

'They surrendered.'

'And you, why didn't you pack in with the rest?'

'Don't know.' The dusky 'South African' shrugged easily. 'I don't think I'd fancy all that Dutch food in captivity. That raw herring they eat all the time. Wouldn't be my beer.'

Otto shook his head. 'Oh, my aching back, I think the whole shitting world is crazy! Do you know what just happened to me? I—' He stopped short. What was the use?

'Could be,' the dusky one said. 'What's the drill now, *Sonderfuhrer*?'

Otto's first reaction was to say, 'We're off. Right quick.' Then he remembered the sneer on the big Dutch bastard's face and the lethal way he had wielded that shitting sword of his. Suddenly he was overcome with a burning rage and a desire for revenge. He'd dearly love to kick van Dongeren in his fat aristocratic behind. But how was he going to do it?

'We could try and rescue the boys,' the dusky one broke into his angry reverie.

'*The boys!* Why, they're always calling you 'nigger' and 'kaffir' and the like,' Otto said in surprise. 'Why should you rescue snotty shits like that?'

'Oh, I don't know,' the 'South African' replied. 'Just their type of humour. I mean we're all Germans really, even if my old lady did tend to walk around Windhoek with her tits showing and her shopping basket on her head – if the old man didn't catch her first.' He frowned a little at the memory. 'She was very sunburnt too.'

'I bet!' Otto said. 'But how could we do it? Neither of us has got a popgun.'

'There's still the tank.'

'Of course!' Otto exclaimed. 'The tin can! I'd forgotten all about that.'

'I haven't,' the dusky one said stoutly. 'I quite liked driving the thing. I think I might even put in for a transfer to the Armoured Corps when we get back.' He sounded as if he really meant it.

'Shit!' Otto said. 'The only thing I'm transferring to when this little lot is over is to the Pay Corps! Now come, I've got a plan, Let's find the tin can . . .'

As usual Dirk had made his appearance at the wrong time. He had come hammering at her bedroom door just as she was whipping the wet cat into that last mad gallop that would have sent it past the winning post in a final exciting, panting frenzy. It was typical of him; he had no thought for anyone else but himself.

Now he was standing there, shifting awkwardly from one foot to the other like an overgrown schoolboy, his lips red with what looked like blood – probably he'd bumped into a door; he was that clumsy – looking at her as if she were not wearing any underthings below her robe, which, of course she realised, was quite true.

She extended her hand. Bowing low he kissed it, leaving a red circle on the white skin. 'How was the war?' she asked for want of something better to say. She supposed officers liked being asked such things.

'Oh, we lost it, actually,' he said somewhat sadly and then he brightened up. 'But we made some of those *Moffen* swine pay for it down there just now, what?'

She ignored his childish enthusiasm. 'At least you'll be able to get out of that ghastly uniform,' she said. 'Green doesn't suit you one bit.'

'Yes, I suppose you're right, my beloved,' he conceded. 'Now one can get back to some real peacetime soldiering at the Palace. I should imagine that the Queen will—' He stopped short and stared at the white bundle that lay in the centre of the rumpled bed clothes. 'I say, my beloved, aren't those underpants, male underpants?' he exclaimed.

Her hand flew to her mouth as one breast popped out of her gown in her agitation. 'Dirk, you really are the limit! How do you think that male under—' The words froze on her lips, as van Dongeren reached over with the point of his sword and picked them up with it.

Slowly, of their own volition, the underpants unfurled to reveal an eagle, holding a small swastika, with the letters 'W' and 'H' on each side of it, stencilled on the bottom.

'W . . . H . . .' van Dongeren said slowly, almost menacingly, 'Property of the German *Wehrmacht*!' He stared at the pale-faced countess hard, trying to keep his gaze from her naked breast for they had agreed to save 'it' until the Queen approved their marriage. Besides Baron van Dongeren always felt embarrassed when the question of sexuality arose. 'Madame,' he said severely, 'I think you have some explaining to do.'

'Rape,' she said simply. 'What else? After all, I am a van Elst!'

'Oh, my God!' he groaned, his face ashen. Shocked beyond measure he let the sword, with Otto's underpants attached, sink slowly, as if he were lowering a flag in surrender. 'In God's name! Think of my position at Court! What will the Queen say?'

'Exactly,' she agreed in a tiny voice, her gaze fixed on the floor, her shoulders shaking with suppressed laughter.

'Which of the swine was it?' van Dongeren demanded fiercely, glaring at the trembling, unhappy German prisoners lined up against the wall of the Great Hall, hands raised, and surrounded by grim-faced Grenadiers, who prodded them at regular intervals with their bayonets like a hungry man might prod a frying sausage to test whether it was ready for eating.

She lowered her gaze, as if in embarrassment. 'I really didn't see his face, Dirk,' she whispered in a little girl's voice.

'Oh, my darling,' with his free hand he pressed hers reassuringly, 'how you must have suffered.'

'Yes, I did.'

'But you must have some means of identifying the perverted criminal?' he persisted.

'Well, yes, there is one thing I remember about him,' she agreed hesitantly.

'What was it?' he asked eagerly.

'Oh, I couldn't say it aloud, Dirk. That would be too much.' She crooked her finger at him to indicate he should come closer. Stiffly he bent his shaven head and she whispered something in his ear.

Van Dongeren flushed a bright crimson and began spluttering meaningless words through his toothless gums like a drowning man going down for the third and last time. Finally he roared, 'In the name of all that is holy, fancy threatening a mere, innocent girl like you with that! All the same it's one way of apprehending the monster.' He lowered his voice. 'Do you think you'd recognise – it?'

'Oh yes, I'm sure I would,' she said.

Van Dongeren shot her a searching look out of the

corner of his eyes. Suddenly she seemed very eager. Next instant he dismissed the thought as absurd and unworthy. Obviously she was simply overwrought, that was it. It was very understandable after the ordeal she had been through at the hands of that perverted *Moffen* swine. 'Do you think you could go through with it, darling?' he asked anxiously.

'Yes, I'll . . . try,' she answered demurely.

'My God, what a brave little woman you are.' Van Dongeren pressed her hand hard, overcome with an emotion of sentimentality, which was unusual in a man who normally only became emotional about the slaughter of partridges and pheasants, and since 10 May, human beings too. He made his decision. 'Mulder,' he snapped.

The elderly butler clicked rustily to attention. For some reason, he was wearing a fireman's brass helmet and carrying a broom handle as if it were a rifle. 'Sir!' he barked.

'Dismiss the female servants.'

'Sir!' Mulder sprang round and bellowed, as if he were on some monstrous parade-ground and the servants were standing a thousand metres and not ten away from him. 'Female servants . . . female servants, *dis-miss*!'

Reluctantly, muttering angrily to themselves, obviously aware that they were going to miss something that would provide a source of gossip for days to come, they left the Great Hall.

Impatiently van Dongeren waited till they had gone. Finally the door closed behind them and van Dongeren turned to the Germans. '*Hosen runter!*' he commanded severely in German.

The German prisoners stared back at the crimson-faced Dutch officer, as if he had suddenly gone crazy. Opposite them the countess licked her lips, a sudden greedy look in her eyes.

Furiously the Baron waved his sword and the NCO in charge of the prisoners pulled back the bolt of his rifle significantly. The prisoners' faces turned white with fear. Reluctantly they started to lower their hands.

Van Dongeren repeated his order.

Mystified and scared, the Brandenburgers started to fumble with their braces and buttons.

A minute later they stood there unhappily, trousers around their ankles to reveal long droopy underpants that hung over skinny, pale legs.

Van Dongeren hesitated.

The countess beat him to it. 'The other things will have to go too, Dirk, if I am to identify the . . . er . . . culprit.'

'Of course, you brave little woman,' he said.'All right, now your underpants!'

There was a murmur of rebellion from the prisoners and Mulder brought up his broom handle smartly, crying, 'One false move and you're dead!'

Miserably the prisoners dropped their underpants and stood there, slightly crouched, with their hands spread across their genitals protectively.

'Nasty business this,' van Dongeren muttered to himself and strode closer to the unhappy Germans.

'Now listen, you wretches, on the command "one"!' he barked, 'you will remove your hands from your . . . er . . . things. On the command "two", you will replace them! There will be no lewd remarks, nor obscene looks. Is that clear?' He swung his sword through the air dangerously close to the first man and there was a frightened, hasty chorus of, 'Yes'.

'Good.' He swung round. Countess van Elst's eyes were glittering strangely, he couldn't help thinking. 'Are you ready, my dear?' he asked.

She nodded, apparently too affected to be able to speak.

A little embarrassed by having to do such a thing in public, he took her in his arms tenderly and gave her a little hug, before releasing her, face flushed and confused. 'If you feel faint, my dear,' he said huskily, 'just close your eyes for a moment and think of our dear

Queen. It will help you to do your duty, as she has always done.'

'I understand,' she replied, finding her voice at last. '*Noblesse oblige*.'

They advanced to the first unhappy prisoner, a tall skinny fellow with bad breath. 'One!' van Dongeren commanded.

The German raised his hands.

The countess gave a little gaze and lifting her hand to her eyes, peered through her fingers like someone looking through a venetian blind. 'No,' she said after a moment's scrutiny, and van Dongeren could have sworn at that moment that she sounded disappointed. Perhaps, he told himself, she now realised she must continue with this terrible ordeal. 'Two!' he commanded and the tall German clapped his hands possessively over his genitals once more, as if he would never let go of them ever again.

Slowly they started to pass down the line of prisoners. Van Dongeren standing at the countess's side thought she was being a little too slow, taking a great deal of time to scrutinise each man's organs, but then he told himself the van Elsts had always been famous in the Dutch aristocracy for their thoroughness. After all the family motto was 'to the bitter end'.

Halfway down the line stood the shortest of the prisoners, known to his NCOs in the *Brandenburg Regiment* as 'short-arse' or 'four-eyes' on account of his thick-rimmed glasses; though in happier days those of his comrades who had seen him in action in Duren's official Army brothel – 'other ranks only up to and including the rank of corporal' – had privately titled him, 'the African Elephant', and it wasn't on account of his prominent nose.

Van Dongeren sniffed as he saw the fat little German with the bent shoulders of an obviously sedentary worker. 'Hardly the type, my dear,' he said, 'to commit a dastardly crime of that nature. Shall we pass on?'

'No,' she commanded with surprising firmness.

'Dirk, we have to do this thing systematically . . . to protect the innocent.'

'Yes, of course,' he agreed hastily. 'Good thinking, my dear.' He looked down at the German who was not much larger than a dwarf. 'One!' he commanded.

Peering up at them owlishly through his thick-lensed glasses, the German raised his pudgy hands.

At van Dongeren's side, the Countess gasped and seemed to sway. Hastily he caught her arm. 'Steady, my dear,' he said urgently. 'Don't faint now when this terrible ordeal is almost over. Do—' he stopped short and followed the direction of her transfixed gaze.

'Good God on high!' he exclaimed in astonishment. 'Is all that . . . yours?'

'Can't help it, sir,' the little man said. 'Born that way. That's why I'm so round-shouldered. The weight you understand, sir.' He smiled up at an open-mouthed van Dongeren winningly.

'Why, it's simply disgusting! It would be impossible for you ever to wear shorts with that . . . thing,' Van Dongeren stuttered, trying not to hear the countess's heavy breathing at his side. He hoped she was not going to swoon now when it was almost over; he couldn't face this highly embarrassing business once again.

'Yes, sir. It was a bit of a nuisance in Jo'burg in the hot season. Occasionally people did stop in the streets when I went by on my bike in shorts. But then,' he added, 'they were mostly Kaffirs, and as you perhaps know, sir, any little thing will set those black heathens off talking?' He beamed at van Dongeren.

'*Little!*' he choked and then swallowing hard turned to the countess. 'Well?' he demanded, trying not to see the strange look on her beautiful face and the hard glitter in her eyes.

'Well, what?' she whispered, her voice strained and remote, not taking her gaze off that monstrous thing for one instant.

'Was it him?' he snapped.

She swallowed hard. 'I can't be quite sure,' she said.

Losing patience with her a little, van Dongeren took her arm and said urgently, 'Come on, my dear, let's move on and have done with it.'

'No, no,' she said determinedly, still not removing her gaze, while the near-dwarf smiled at her hypnotised face like a fat, happy owl, 'we must make quite, quite sure!'

Van Dongeren let his shoulders slump in defeat.

SEVEN

'Hold tight, *Sonderfuhrer*!' the dusky 'South African' sang out, '*here we go*!'

He put his foot down hard on the gas pedal and thrust the two control sticks forward.

With a roar, the tank started to crawl up the high ornamental staircase that led to the main door of the castle, while Otto hung on grimly to the breech of the 37mm cannon, praying that they would make it.

With a great metallic slap the tracks surmounted the top step and hit the stone once more.

The dusky one revved the engine madly. 'Now for the door,' he whooped, obviously delighted with his performance. 'At it like Marshal Blucher!'

The tank shot forward, hit the door with a loud rending sound, and next instant was careering through a mess of flying wood straight into the broad corridor that led to the Great Hall. Infected by the 'South African's' enthusiasm, Otto pulled wildly at the firing bar and wished the next instant he hadn't. The gun exploded with a tremendous roar and in that confined space it sounded as if the very world was coming to an end. The pictures of the nineteenth century worthies slithered to the floor, pewter plates and ornamental jugs came raining down crazily and, to their front, the door of the Great Hall disintegrated, peppering the tank's steep glacis plate with flying wood splinters.

'Whoopee!' the driver yelled exuberantly. 'That's the

stuff to give the troops, *Sonderfuhrer*!' Churning the remnants of priceless Ming vases under the tank's flailing tracks, window after window exploding outwards with that tremendous noise as they rattled by, the driver swung into the Great Hall and braked the tank to a surprised stop.

'*What in three devils*—' Otto began and stopped short.

No wonder the driver had braked so abruptly!

On the floor, hugging the carpet, lay their comrades, naked rumps exposed, save for a dwarflike fellow, grinning all over his owlish face standing there in the middle of the Hall displaying himself for the benefit of a dreamy-faced Countess, while the Dutch Grenadiers scattered for cover. 'Jesus wept,' he gasped, 'what's been going on here?'

'Looks to me, as if they were playing some sort of game,' the driver replied cheerfully, recovered from his shock now. 'Touch and Tell, or something like that.'

'Touch that thing once and she'd be able to *tell* all right,' Otto said grimly, noting just how excitedly the countess was breathing, completely oblivious to the dramatic arrival of the tank, her cheeks flushed hecticly, her whole being concentrated on that one ugly thing.

'Look out!' the driver cried in sudden alarm.

Otto swung his gaze from the strange couple in the centre of the Hall. Coming from the cover of an armchair behind which he had hidden in the first fright of the tank's bursting through the door, was the Dong, waving his sword again, scarred face livid with rage, meaningless phrases tumbling out of his toothless mouth.

'Oh shit,' Otto moaned, 'not Douglas Fairbanks again!'

The Dutchman grabbed hold of the front of the glacis plate and prepared to haul himself up. Otto reacted quickly. He pressed the button which activated the turret mechanism. With a soft hiss the turret swung round. Van Dongeren howled with pain as the gun barrel hit him in the midriff and swept him over the side. He fell to the floor arms and legs flailing.

'Good for you, Otto!' the driver yelled with delight. 'You don't mind if I use your first name, I hope?' he added hastily.

'This is supposed to be a war, not a shitting dancing school! Call me what you like.'

The Dong was up on his feet again, slashing and hacking at the tank's steel side in crazed fury, cursing horribly now.

'Now it's struck thirteen!' Otto yelled, sick of the big fool of a cheesehead. He jerked the lever which depressed the cannon and in the next instant had pressed the turret button once more. Down below the red-faced Dong continued to cut away, the blade of his sword jagged like a carving knife now, crying to himself, 'I'll get into you! By God I will, if it's the last thing I do . . . You can't hide in there for ever—'

The gun hit him a relatively gentle blow on the side of his shaven head – that is, if one can call twenty-two hundredweight of milled steel striking one 'gentle'. His eyes crossed abruptly and his legs began to give way beneath him like those of a newly born foal. Slowly the sword slipped from his suddenly nerveless fingers and rattled to the floor. A moment later he followed it.

Mulder, the butler, was the first to recover from the shock of that strange little battle. Marching smartly across the room, he picked up the Dutchman's ruined sword and reached it up, hilt-first, to Otto in the turret He bowed stiffly from the waist and said in that solemn voice of his, '*Herr Leutnant*, herewith I hand you the blade of Major, the Baron van Dongeren. It is my unpleasant duty to inform you that by this act the Queen's Grenadiers have surrendered.' He gave another bow and started walking backwards awkwardly, as if he were in the presence of royalty, while Otto watched him open-mouthed, sword clutched in his hand.

On all sides the Grenadiers started to crawl from their hiding-places behind the furniture and the wall carpets and began to pile their weapons in a neat heap as the Brandenburgers, red-faced and still awed by that strange short-arm inspection, started to draw up their trousers in silence, avoiding each other's gazes.

Still the dwarflike chap and the countess continued to stare at each other, until finally Otto called, 'All right, young lovers. It's all over for today . . . Hey you,' he bellowed angrily, when the little man still hadn't moved, 'get that horrible thing covered up, or I swear by the Great Whore of Buxtehude, I'll saw it off personally with this!' He waved the sword menacingly.

That terrible threat finally did the trick. Hurriedly the little man ripped up his pants and started to fasten his flies with thick clumsy fingers. '*I'm coming, Sonderfuhrer*,' he cried nervously. '*I'm coming* . . .'

'Oh no you aint,' Otto said scornfully, as the countess started to shake all over, her eyes revolving in their sockets, as if she were going to have an epilectic fit, 'but I know somebody who is . . .'

Four hours later, the Brandenburgers led by Otto in the tank and their prisoners of the Queen's Grenadiers reached the German frontline. They were greeted with cheers by the infantry dug in in the wet dreary Dutch field, slapped on the back and generally treated like heroes.

Generously the young infantry captain in charge offered to take over their prisoners for them so that the weary Brandenburgers could get some sleep there and then, but after ascertaining the Gennep Bridge was well behind the German frontline now, Otto declined politely. He wasn't taking any more chances; you could never be sure what new dangers might occur at the front.

After a hasty meal of pea soup from the unit's goulash-cannon and after borrowing some diesel for the tank, they set off again with the captain's final admiring words ringing in their ears. 'By all that is holy, you grand fellows of the Brandenburg never know when to give up. Right on to the bitter end. Nothing can go wrong for the Fatherland as long as it produces brave chaps like you.' Unfeelingly Otto farted.

Two hours after that they arrived at the Gennep Bridge guarded by what was left of the Count's force and the reinforcements led by Maps, who was now armed with a large disinfectant spray, his back bowed under an enormous pack, containing white delousing powder.

Again their welcome was tremendous and the Count immediately made an emotional impromptu speech, tears running down his plump cheeks as he did so, praising their spirit of self-sacrifice and 'excessive devotion to duty' and expressing his 'heartfelt relief' that their lives had been spared for 'Folk, Fatherland and Fuhrer', while an anxious Maps hovered around the new arrivals making excited little pumping gestures.

'Christ, I'm almost beginning to believe him myself,' Otto whispered in disgust to the grinning driver.

'Oh, I don't know,' he said. 'It sounds real enough to me. Can't harm anyone when the truth is bent a bit, like that. Medals mean gash,' he added with surprising directness for him.

Otto looked at him in surprise.

Finally the Count was finished and a delighted Maps was allowed to execute his new office.

'Delousing officer,' the Count explained, his arm around Otto's shoulders possessively, as Maps poked his spray first in the new arrivals' sleeves and then in their flies, bravely pumping so that coughing men were soon wreathed in clouds of white powder. 'New order from the High Command. Every unit has got to have one. Apparently our people in England have reported the English have been experimenting with poisoned lice. A sort of venereal crab or something like that. Gives you VD without intercourse. Very frightening, if it's true. Anyway,' he shrugged, 'it keeps him out of mischief and it's better than those little green men with the metallic antennae, eh?'

Otto laughed and for a moment or two they were silent, as they watched the Grenadiers file into a barbed-wire cage, led by a dejected van Dongeren, a great green-and-black shiner decorating his sullen scarred face now.

'Must have put up a terrific fight, Otto,' the Count commented. 'But the best man won, eh, as the English say.'

Otto gave a non-committal grunt.

'Cheer up,' the Count urged, mistaking his silence for dejection, 'the whole front is abuzz with your exploits now. How you took on the élite of the Dutch Army and beat it and warded off the counter-attack. Everyone knows how you saved the bridgehead, perhaps even the whole invasion of Holland.' He beamed at Otto. 'My boy, don't you understand – you're a hero!'

Otto yawned. 'All I know Meadow, is that I'm shitting well falling asleep on my feet. Hardly got a wink last night. I could sleep for a month!'

The Count was immediately solicitous. 'Of course, Otto. I understand you very well. The strain must have been tremendous, fighting off the enemy like that all night!'

'I wouldn't exactly call it the enemy,' Otto said cautiously.

The Count beamed. 'That's the spirit, Otto! Now we've won we can afford to be generous to them, can't we?' He indicated the Grenadiers, now locked up inside the wire cage, seemingly doing some sort of ceremonial drill under the watchful one-eye of van Dongeren.

Otto yawned and stared at the Dutchmen without enthusiasm, his eyelids feeling as if there were heavy weights attached to them.

But Otto was fated not to be able to go to sleep just yet. Just at that moment the howl of a klaxon horn at the other side of the stretch of stagnant water roused soldiers everywhere out of the late-afternoon lethargy.

Otto turned to stare with the rest. An armoured car, its gun moving suspiciously from left to right like the snout of some predatory monster was coming slowly up the approach road to the bridge. Behind came six motor-cycle outriders in black uniform, sitting proudly on their gleaming machines, one white-gloved hand on their hips, posing affectedly like the professional warm brothers at Berlin's Anhalter Station, for whom now the Witch did their washing. After the outriders, drove a huge black 12-cylinder Mercedes, its running boards jammed with black-clad giants, hands clapped on their pistol holsters, eyes darting everywhere suspiciously.

Cheers began to ripple along both sides of the road and half-naked soldiers waved the towels on which they had been sunbathing or ran to grab their box cameras to take a picture before it was too late. Slowly as the little procession approached the bridge, two words ran from mouth to mouth before it reached the Brandenburgers' camp just in time to explode there with the impact of a 88mm shell. '*Der Fuhrer* . . . DER FUHRER!'

At Otto's side, the Count tensed. Otto flashed him a look. The middle-aged aristocrat had gone very pale suddenly; then he recovered himself and hurriedly buttoned up his collar as the procession started to roll to a stop. Gripping his overlong sabre, he marched proudly over to where the Mercedes had come to a halt, its occupants immediately springing to their feet and focusing their field glasses in a dozen different directions for the benefit of the UFA cameramen who had appeared from nowhere, their cameras whirring.

Otto recognised most of the crooks. There was Hitler, of course, busy patting the head of a blond little boy who had been produced from one of the following cars especially for this occasion. The German public knew that their Fuhrer loved little boys. Behind him there was Goering looking like a comic-opera field marshal, every single millimetre of his enormous belly and chest covered in medals so that he sparkled in the late-afternoon sun like a Christmas tree ablaze with candles on *Heiligabend**. Goering towered over Himmler, the head of the SS, a sombre, chinless man peering anxiously through his pince-nez at the cameramen like a book-

* Christmas Eve.

keeper worrying about the cost of everything. Finally he gave a little sigh as an expansive Goering, a big grin on his berouged face, started tossing out packets of cigarettes to the happy soldiers, and concentrated his gaze thoughtfully on the Grenadiers who were standing rigidly to attention, as if they were back on duty in front of the Queen's Palace in the Hague.

The Count halted and raised his sabre to his forehead in a sparkle of silver. In a loud clear voice, he reported in the traditional manner, as if he had been playing soldier all his life: 'One officer, four NCOs and fifty men of Regiment Brandenburg present and correct, *mein Fuhrer!*'

Hitler peered down at him a little short-sightedly. 'Ah, my brave Brandenburgers,' he said, obviously not knowing who they were and what they had achieved. He smiled somewhat helplessly.

Behind him one of the gigantic SS aides bent down and whispered swiftly into his ear. 'Captured bridge by *coup de main* . . . Fought off counter-attack . . . Decimated élite Dutch regiment . . . name Count von der Weide . . . Unit . . . *Abwehr* . . .'

Hitler nodded his thanks, his face looking more certain. 'Ah, my dear Count,' he said looking down at the Count. 'We are pleased with you, exceedingly pleased. What a tremendous achievement! Capturing this so vital bridge in such a bold, original manner.'

The Count started to go crimson with pleasure and his knees trembled slightly.

'How brave your chaps must be to have taken on such well-trained troops and beaten them to a standstill, in spite of your small numbers!' He clicked his fingers imperiously.

Behind him the gigantic aide thrust two baskets piled high with decorations in front of the Fuhrer. 'First or second, sir?' he asked, as if he were offering the Leader a choice of chocolates.

'First, of course,' Hitler snapped. 'After all, he is an aristocrat.'

'Of course, sir.'

Solemnly the Fuhrer took the Iron Cross First Class out of the smaller basket and said, 'Herewith by the power granted to me as Fuhrer of the German Folk and Commander-in-Chief of the Great German Army, I bestow on you, my dear Count von der Weide, the order of the Iron Cross, First Class.'

Proudly the Count offered his chest to the man he had wanted to assassinate only a few short days before and suppressed the little yelp of pain just in time as the pin nicked his flesh. '*Danke, mein Fuhrer*,' he barked instead in the approved military fashion, face a lobster-red with pride.

'Now, one of your men,' Hitler said, 'a common soldier, always looks good in the newsreels, you know.'

'*Jawohl, mein Fuhrer*,' the Count answered. 'Sonderfuhrer Stahl, Otto.'

'Birthplace?'

'Berlin, sir.'

'Father and mother?'

'I think that his father is dead.'

'Good, Count, that will do,' Hitler said and nodded to the aide.

'Second class,' he ordered.

A moment later a surprised Otto stood rigidly to attention in front of Adolf Hitler, while the cameras whirred and the photographers jostled each other to get a good shot of this handsome young hero from Berlin. The capital was a very big city and a photograph of a local boy would sell a lot of newspapers.

Hitler pinned the Iron Cross on Otto's chest and said, 'Berlin will be proud of you, Stahl. But then it was to be expected, eh. *Nomen est omen*, that's Latin,' he added hastily. 'It means that—'

'I've heard it before, sir,' Otto said, reasoning that as a hero he could even interrupt the *Fuhrer*.

'Of course, just because you're a working-class boy, it doesn't mean you're stupid. If only your dear dead father could have been alive to have experienced this great moment,' he continued, while Otto listened in growing astonishment. How could he know about Berlin and the missing old man? Was it true, as it was rumoured, that the Fuhrer had the power of second-sight? How else could he have known?

'But at least, your humble, hard-working, honest mother will have that pleasure,' Hitler said and patted Otto's helmet, and in an instant Otto knew that the Fuhrer was not infallible after all. No one in his right mind would ever call the Witch humble, hard-working and especially, *honest*!

A few moments later the cavalcade was off again, with Himmler, whose skinny black-clad chest was devoid of any decorations, watching the baskets filled with Iron Crosses with greedy eyes, while the gigantic aide counted them.

'Hope they've got enough for the rest of the day?' Otto commented sourly out of the side of his mouth to the Count, while the Mercedes gathered speed and Maps, who had been holding his spray with itchy fingers, waiting excitedly for this moment, raised it and puffed a cloud of delousing powder after the Fuhrer.

'What a man!' the Count breathed as the Mercedes finally vanished round the bend and they could relax. 'Those dynamic eyes! That noble brow! Every millimetre a great leader of men!' He sighed at the fond memory. 'For a few moments, Otto, we were in the presence of genius. Now you can tell your children, nay even your grandchildren, that you shook the hand of Adolf Hitler himself.'

'He doesn't shit through the ribs, you know?' was Otto's sole comment. Unpinning the Iron Cross and stowing it carelessly in his pocket, he trudged to the tank and lay down wearily in the shade it afforded. A few minutes later he was snoring loudly, out to the world, the Battle for Holland totally forgotten.

On tiptoe the Count stole over to him and stared down at a red-faced, open-mouthed Otto. 'The warrior who has fought the good fight,' he said softly and touched his medal as if to reassure himself that it was still there. 'A man of the people – a hero!' Gently he unbuckled the bed-roll on the side of the tank and draped the blankets over the sleeping soldier. He beamed at Otto who was sawing wood with ever increasing vigour now, his upper lip making strange little trembling movements. 'Good night, sweet prince,' he whispered in English and then tiptoed away, leaving the hero to his dreams and eternal glory . . .

EIGHT

The Count paused dramatically at the door of the company office. Today for the first time in weeks he no longer wore his tight-fitting elegant cavalry uniform, complete with Iron Cross. Instead he was dressed in a rough working-man's *joppe*, leather breeches, and a battered old green felt hat, complete with feather. He looked like a refugee from the backwoods of Bavaria.

Otto took his feet off the desk in astonishment. 'What happened?' he demanded.

The Count swallowed miserably. 'I've taken a dive.'

'A dive?'

'Yes.' He took off his absurd Bavarian hat and mopped his damp brow. 'Wasn't it Sophocles who once said: 'To die would be good, but never to have been born would have been better?' He sighed and slumped forlornly in a free chair.

Outside in the Brandenburgers' barracks at Duren, the new recruits were hopping around the square at the command of the training sergeants like large clumsy grey squirrels, wearing helmets.

'Well, come on, cough it out,' Otto snapped.

'Otto there have been developments, terrible developments. The Gestapo will be after me – and you – soon. I thought it better to take a dive now while I still had time. Father Christmas thought the same.'

'Gestapo?' Otto echoed in amazement, 'what's going on?'

'It's that Grenadiers' officer Dirk van Dongeren, he's volunteered for the Armed SS, and Himmler has accepted.'

'That doesn't surprise me one bit,' Otto said darkly. 'Now he'll be able to play with that shitting penknife of his all the time. But what's that got to do with the Gestapo?'

'Of course, Himmler's eager to have him because van Dongeren is well connected at Court. Himmler's hoping the Dutch aristocracy will lend a bit of class to the SS. I suppose he's still missing Prince Bernhard.'

'Oh get on with it!'

'Well, naturally van Dongeren had to be vetted by SS Intelligence first. His personal reasons for joining the SS. I think there's some woman trouble behind it really—'

Otto looked hard at the miserable-faced Count, but said nothing, wondering what was coming now. Outside on the square, a grim-faced NCO was standing menacingly just behind a trembling bespectacled recruit, crying, 'Am I hurting you, *Herr Professor*?'

'No,' the academic quavered, wondering what was to come. 'No, Sergeant.'

'Then I shitting well should be, because I'm standing on your shitty curly locks!' the NCO exploded in red-faced artificial fury. 'Get that shitting hair sabred off by sixteen hundred hours this afternoon!'

'But that's not all. He told the Intelligence chaps what happened at the castle that night, everything,' he added unhappily, 'how the lot of you surrendered without a fight. Apparently there is even some talk of the rape of a high-born Dutch lady, the mistress of the castle, I think.'

'*Rape!*' Otto cried indignantly and laughed hollowly. 'I could tell you a tale or two about who was soddingly well raped.'

But the Count wasn't listening. 'At all events, our decorations have been withdrawn, we gained them under false pretences, according to Herr Himmler, and he's insisting on a court-martial for the lot of us!'

'Bollocks!'

'Yes, you're to be charged with desertion on the field of battle. Very serious. Death penalty, you know. The wages of sin are death, eh?' He smiled a little sadly at Otto, whose brain was racing furiously at this new frightening development. Finally he said, 'Sometimes, Count, I don't know why whoever organised this rotten world arranged for men to have anything to do with women.'

'Don't be bitter, Otto,' the Count said, trying to cheer him up. 'I'll come up with a plan. Somehow or other I'll get us out of this mess. Trust old Meadow. Oh no, can't use that code-name any more,' he added hastily. 'Call me Count, all that spy business is, I'm afraid, over now.'

'All right, Count, but don't you worry about making a plan. This time, I'll do it,' he jerked a thumb aggressively at his own chest. 'In August 1939, I decided I didn't want to fight for Hitler. It doesn't matter now why. So I get myself a job in the *Westwall*, nice and remote and away from it all, so I thought. But then a crazy NCO's wife lands me in the shit and I take up with a little Belgie crook – and eventually land in the ordure again. You come along and do the same.' The Count looked pained, but said nothing, letting Otto get it off his chest. 'And what do I end up doing, fighting for Hitler after all and getting a medal for doing so.' Otto frowned hard at the thought, shaking his head, as if he could hardly believe it had happened. 'No, Count, if I'm going to land in the shit once again, then it's going to be my own fault. Understand?'

'Naturally I understand, my dear boy,' the Count said hastily. 'But what is your plan exactly?'

'I don't know at this moment, but I'll think of something. But first I need money, lots of it,' he made a counting gesture with his finger and thumb.

The Count frowned. ''fraid I'm broke, Otto,' he said. 'The von der Weiden have always lived well, indeed some would say in a profligate manner, and for the time being I am unable to draw on Father Christmas's secret slush fund.'

Otto considered. Outside the recruits were chanting the cadence as they marched up and down the square in the August heat, 'Left . . . right, left . . . right,' little pieces of red gun-flannel fluttering on their left thumbs as they swung their arms. Otto shook his head in disbelief. What a world it was where grown men had to have a piece of cloth tied to their thumbs to remind them which was their left hand. Crazy, absolutely crazy! It deserved to be taken for a ride.

'Count,' he said suddenly, 'how many recruits do you think the barracks holds now?'

He shrugged. 'Eight hundred to a thousand, perhaps. Why do you ask, Otto?'

Otto didn't answer. His mind was doing a quick calculation. Then he said, 'It's payday for the recruits tomorrow, isn't it, Count?'

'Yes, wh—'

'No names, no pack drill, Count,' Otto cut him short quickly. 'Hang on here for fifteen minutes and then be prepared to move – *quick*!' And with that he was gone, leaving the Count to his thoughts, which were not happy, and the monotonous voice of some gunnery instructor outside, naming the parts with the excessive detail of his kind, 'Now this is the sling . . . Now this is the stock . . . Now this is . . .'

Exactly fifteen minutes later, Otto returned, his eyes gleaming with excitement, his face flushed, clutching a heavy carrier-bag to his chest. 'Come on, Count,' he gasped, 'dig it out of the orifice! We've only got thirty minutes to catch the Aachen-Berlin express, first class, of course.'

'First class . . . Aachen-Berlin express?' the Count stuttered. 'What . . . why. . . ?'

Otto opened the bag for an instant.

The Count gasped. It was full to the brim of green five-mark notes. He stood there, unable to speak, like a stranded fish in its last throes.

'Regimental payroll,' Otto explained and reached for his cap.

'Keep those tosspots out of the whorehouses down in the old town this weekend, I'll be bound! Besides, doesn't the old bonemender always say that the one-handed widow is safer than getting a dose of clap. Why,' he smiled triumphantly at a still spluttering Count von der Weide, 'we're doing those young fellows down there a real favour . . . Come on! *Los, nach Berlin* . . .'

NINE

'*Aufmachen!*' the harsh voice thundered outside.

The Witch hobbled to the window of her little Berlin flat and looked cautiously out from behind the lace curtain.

'Well?' Otto demanded, while the Count cowered next to him on the shabby sofa, already suspecting the worse.

'Headhunters!' she said.

'Shit!' Otto cursed. 'We've only just got here and they're already sending the military police after us.'

'Don't shit yersen,' his mother replied easily. 'My guess is that it's just routine. I'll look after it.' Hastily she took out her new false teeth and her raddled old face fell in hideously.

'What are you going to do, you old bag?' Otto asked, while the Count stared at her aghast, the hammering down below forgotten for a moment with the shock of that terrible apparition.

There was worse to come. Cackling crazily, the Witch slipped her nightgown over her head with surprising speed for such an old woman to reveal her naked, skinny old whore's body in all its hideousness. 'Leave it to me, Otto,' she said, giving him a toothless smile and grabbed the big bottle from which she had just poured him and the Count a glass of beer. Then she was gone and the Count gave a gasp of relief. 'Otto,' he sobbed, 'what on earth is she going to do?'

'God knows!' Otto answered.

'*Heaven, arse and cloudburst!*' the bigger of the two MPs with the silver crescent of his calling around his thick neck, gasped and staggered at the door, as if some invisible fist had punched him. 'What in the name of Heaven is *that*?'

Next to him his comrade nearly dropped his rifle with shock.

'*Na meine Süssen!*' the Witch croaked, as she stood there at the top of the stairs, her dugs bouncing from her skinny yellow belly, as she ground her hips in an obscene parody of her old calling 'Come on up. There's plenty of sauce.' She raised the bottle to reveal the tuft of thick grey hair under her armpit, and added in what she supposed was a seductive whisper. 'I can show yer little tricks yer've never dreamed of.' She started to walk down the stairs, swinging her bony hips and ogling them hungrily.

The two headhunters backed away in horror. 'Get off,' the bigger of the two cried in terror, 'don't you dare lay a finger on me!' His big hand held out as if to fend her off, he started to stumble towards the open door.

'For Chrissake, don't leave me, Heinz!' the other one screamed. 'She'll get me!'

Halfway down the stairs, the Witch cackled hideously and spread her stick-like legs. 'Come on boys, look what I can offer yer!' That did it. The two military policemen fled . . .

'So you're on the run, Otto,' she said proudly, half an hour and two bottles of *Kindl* beer later. 'Now I really know you're my son.' She reached out a claw and attempted to stroke his cheek.

Otto ducked hastily and said, 'For God's sake, put on a dress, will you! Any minute now you're going to dangle a tit in my beer.'

'You're not very grateful to your old mother, I must say,' she grumbled sulkily and got up to put on a dress.

'But you take after your father. Not only in looks, he was mean too.'

'How would you know?' Otto quipped. 'You only ever saw him once – and that was in the dark.'

Dutifully she pulled the dress over her head and made herself another enormous bowl of *Berliner Weisser*, a mixture of beer, lemonade and raspberry juice, while the Count breathed a sigh of relief that this extraordinary woman, whom Otto called mother, and who was going to shelter them in Berlin, was dressed again.

'What yer going to do?' Otto asked, 'drink it or have a bath in it? And come to think of it, that wouldn't be a bad idea. There's a terrible pong in here.'

'Don't begrudge yer poor old mother a little pleasure,' the Witch answered and, lifting the bowl with both claws, drained a litre in one go. She gasped and wiped the foam off her wrinkled lips. 'Ah, that's better!' she said businesslike now. 'Now then, what's up? What do you want the Witch to do for you, Otto – and of course your nice friend?' She ogled the Count, naked lechery in her ancient eyes, and the Count shuddered.

'Stop that carry-on!' Otto said sharply. 'I need yer broomstick. I want to get out of the Reich, at least for the time being. I think the Gestapo is after us, and the Army is anyway, as you've just heard.'

'The Gestapo – that bunch of barnshitters,' she said contemptuously. 'I wouldn't worry about them much, Otto.'

'You wouldn't. You'd frighten even Heydrich* out of his drawers!'

She cackled, 'That's a good one, Otto.'

'But if they catch *me* and my comrade here, we're for the chop. Turnip off!' He made a slicing gesture with his extended hand. Next to him on the couch, the Count blanched.

'"The guillotine is a machine which takes off the head in a flash",' the Witch said in an affected, upper-class

* The feared head of the Gestapo and SS Intelligence Service.

accent, '"so that the victim feels nothing – save a pleasant sense of coolness around the neck region." That's what the judge said to your grandfather,' she continued relapsing into her normal, thick Berlin working-class dialect, 'maternal of course, before he ordered him to have his turnip sliced off. I was only a slip of a girl at the time but I remember it as if it was yesterday. Things like that stay with yer, don't they, er Count?' She smiled winningly at him.

'Yes, yes, Madame Stahl,' he stuttered hurriedly.

'In three devils' name, change the subject, will you!' Otto said in exasperation. 'Now who do you know who can help us? . . . Silly old bag.'

Thoughtfully the Witch nibbled at her nails, pausing occasionally to spit out the dirt that lay there, muttering to herself at intervals, then shaking her head, as if she were rejecting whoever had just come into her mind. Finally she looked up and said: 'Farthmann.'

'I beg your pardon, Madame Stahl?' the Count exclaimed.

She ignored him. 'Frieda Farthmann, Otto. She's your woman.'

'That crooked old bitch!' Otto said. He remembered his mother's old crony from his boyhood. They had pounded the pavements together for years, but Frieda had always been an enterprising little crook on the side too. He recalled the times she had trapped the sparrows in the *Tiergarten*, painted them yellow, and sold them to gullible middle-class housewives in Berlin-Dahlem as canaries. Then she'd done quite well smuggling drugs, tobacco and the like into the wealthier prisoners in Spandau Jail by means of the silver cassiber she kept hidden in a more intimate portion of her anatomy. Until one day a whole kilo of cigarette tobacco hidden in the tube had disappeared – with disastrous results. The local 'angel-maker'* had been forced to get it out with his scalpel. Since then she had walked in a strange

* Abortionist.

open-legged gait that had drawn catcalls and cries from fellow pavement-pounders of 'Where yer lost yer nag, Frieda?' – and worse.

'She's in the big time now, since she had her accident and got that fancy compensation.'

'Accident . . . compensation?'

'Yes. Last Christmas she took on a whole company of the *Leibstandarte*.'

'What?' Otto cried incredulously. 'Don't tell me she's still doing the mattress polka? It must have been a couple of centuries ago since she could lift her flipper high enough for a quick knee-trembler in some doorway!'

'Well, anyway she did. Those boys of the SS aren't so fussy you know. They put her in a bath-chair, but they all had to club up one week's pay to compensate her. That's when she went into business. Now she's a lady, got people working for her and everything. She's gone international too.'

'International – what do you mean, you old bag?'

But for once the Witch was silent.

Berlin's *Kurfurstendamm* sparkled in the sun. Everywhere the elegant outdoor cafés were packed with well-dressed women in floral dresses and hats and veils, talking animatedly over their champagne with attentive handsome officers, hung like Christmas trees with the new decorations won in Poland and the West. Smartly dressed soldiers of the garrison strode back and forth in pairs, trying to pick up the shopgirls and the little secretaries who were everywhere, saluting officers and barking military greetings to and fro. Somewhere an Army band played, all crashing cymbals and blaring brass. The very air seemed heavy with victory.

Feeling shabby and out of place in such surroundings, the only civilian there save the supercilious waiters, Otto nursed his cold coffee and wondered if it wouldn't have been better to meet *Frau Direktor*

Farthmann (as she now called herself) back at the Witch's flat. But the Witch would have none of it. 'She's far too grand these days to come here. Besides,' she had added, 'it would be bad for business for her to be seen in Berlin-Wedding, a real working-class place like this!' And so Otto had been forced to make the rendezvous the *Kurfurstendamm*, leaving a worried, very nervous Count with the Witch, who had been growing more and more amorous by the second.

Time passed leadenly and Otto started to wonder if *Frau Direktor* Farthmann had not stood him up. An arrogant waiter strolled by and looked pointedly at his cup. 'Not finished *yet*?' he said.

'I suppose this place is so posh,' Otto sneered, 'that you waiters tip each other.' He stuck out his foot and the arrogant waiter could only save himself from falling by grabbing the next table, thus unfortunately spilling a pot of coffee over the lap of the elegant woman in silk who sat there. Next to her, her companion, a dashing *Luftwaffe* pilot, the Knight's Cross dangling at his neck, withdrew his scalded hand hastily and cursed the waiter.

Otto grinned.

It was just about then that the bath-chair made its appearance in front of the café, pushed by a too-handsome young officer, dressed in a uniform that Otto could not recognise, his olive-skinned face decorated by a thin jet-black moustache which looked as if he might well pencil it on every morning in front of his shaving mirror.

But it was not the young lieutenant who caught and held Otto's attention at that moment, as everywhere awed waiters and officers dashed to move the tables apart to allow the bath-chair to enter. It was the woman sitting in it. Her demeanour was so regal that she might well have been the old Queen of Prussia sitting in her state carriage, with her silver hair piled up like a pagoda. For one long moment an awed Otto could not believe that this was the mother's old crony of her pavement-pounder days, but then that leathery face on which you could have cracked rocks on easily formed a smile of recognition and Frieda Farthmann said, 'Hello Otto, *got yer dong in the old wringer, again eh*!

'Abroad, eh?' *Frau Direktor* Farthmann mused thoughtfully, while the waiters hurried back and forth and Lieutenant Mikos, of the Hungarian Hussars, argued hotly with the waiters about the brand of champagne they were attempting to serve them – for some reason, unknown to Otto, speaking French. '*Non, non pas brut. Madame la Directice, ne boit pas brut. Jamais!*'

'I could set you up in a little thing I've got going in Rumania, Otto,' she said. 'Catholic country. Hence no Parisians. Tremendous market for French ticklers or Berliner Bearhugs – I created that one myself,' she added proudly, 'in Bucharest. Cost a bit though,' she continued, shooting Otto a sharp look. Otto shook his head dubiously. 'No, Frieda, I can't really see myself flogging rubbers to Rumanians somehow.'

'You must realise, Otto,' Frieda lectured, while the waiters finally started to pour the French champagne which Mikos had ordered. 'We Germans control the whole Continent from the Channel to the Vistula, and even these garlic-gobblers like that piece of Hungarian goulash,' she indicated Mikos with her be-ringed finger and the lieutenant, who did not speak a word of German, beamed back at her, 'are well and truly in our sphere of influence. Europe is Germany's oyster now and Frieda Farthmann is gonna grab as many pearls as she can before the market goes bust.' She took a swig of her champagne as if it were the beer she had drunk in her old days as a five-mark pavement-pounder. 'Take my advice, Otto, do the same.' She drained the glass, belched, and held it out for the Hungarian to fill it again.

Hurriedly he did so, attempting to kiss her hand covered with large brown liverspots as he did so.

She withdrew hastily, crying, 'Get off, you filthy shit! God only knows where you had those lips an hour ago.' She winked knowingly at Otto.

Desperately Otto tried to get the raddled, old ex-whore back to the subject of discussion. 'Frieda, I'm out of place here and I think I'd be out of place in . . . er big business. All this,' he waved a hand somewhat helplessly around at the elegant crowd, 'is not my style. Can't you find me something nice and humble abroad where I don't have to tackle this sort of thing?'

Frieda looked at him sternly. 'Otto, don't under-estimate yersen, *ever*! Don't you know by now that the Devil always shits on the biggest heap? . . . All right, how much have you got?' She extended a powdered claw, as if she were back in the *Tiergarten* haggling with some drunken customer about the price of her services against the nearest tree. 'The marie . . . How much?'

Otto told her.

She sniffed. 'Otto, these days, that kind of cabbage doesn't even pay my weekly champus bill. But no matter. I've known yer since yer was as high as three cheeses. I'll help yer.'

'Thanks!' Otto breathed happily, confident now that a transformed Frieda Farthmann would be able to pull it off successfully for him and the Count. 'Where . . . and what?'

'France, Otto,' she declared.

'Oh là, là!' Mikos simpered, obviously understanding the German word. He touched his manicured, lacquered fingers to his lips and said, '*sucre!*'

'You're gonna get yersen a nasty disease doing that one of these days,' Frieda commented obscurely and added, 'I'll let you have one of my Mobile Troop Social and Welfare establishments, officially approved by the German Red Cross, Union of German Mothers, as well as the Winter Relief.' She frowned, 'Of course the territory isn't the best. Just outside Dijon in Occupied France. Country area with a few small towns. But what can you expect, Otto, for that kind of cabbage.'

Otto opened his mouth to speak, but already she was off again.

'But it's nicely out of the way for somebody like you wanting to take a dive. There are enough stubble-hoppers down there to keep you busy and make a few coins – by the way no Frogs. Our rules don't allow it – and I imagine it'll be your kind of social class, you'll be mixing with. Hairy-arsed, working-class squaddies!'

'But what is it, Frieda?' Otto broke in at last.

'Don't you know?'

He shook his head.

'I thought everyone knew what Frieda Farthmann's Mobile Troop Social and Welfare establishments were,' she declared in amazement. 'Had 'em running all over the Reich and German-Occupied Europe since the early summer. Last week the Fuhrer himself inspected the one we've got going in the Berchtesgaden area and gave it his official approval.'

'Shit on the shingle, Frieda!' Otto cried, exasperated beyond measure. 'Will yer just tell me what it is I'm getting into?'

Frau Direktor Farthmann gave Otto the full benefit of her false-toothed smile. 'Why Otto, my darling, a *knocking shop on wheels!*'

ENVOI.

'*Panziena!*' cried Angelo. 'We have stood up to a great deal, we can stand what is still to come, whether it's poverty or plenty. For we have learnt the most useful of all accomplishments, which is to survive.'

Eric Linklater: Private Angelo, 1946

'*A pimp!*' the Count had exclaimed when Otto had first related to him the outcome of his discussions with *Frau Direktor* Frieda Farthmann. 'But my dear boy, you can't expect a von der Weide to pimp!'

But when he had seen the great lumbering converted furniture van, pulled by eight dray horses from a Berlin brewery, its sides decorated with suitably patriotic slogans such as '*Everything for the Fuhrer*' and '*Our Wheels Roll For Victory*', he had become a little less aggrieved. He had condescended to examine the interior, divided up into four little cubicles, containing a cot, a wash-basin, and six hundred-piece cartons of contraceptives, type 'Volcano', for which *Frau Direktor* Farthmann had demanded the concession. 'Best German workmanship, Otto. Nothing ersatz about those rubbers, the real stuff. Got to look after our brave boys, you know.'

The 'girls' themselves had done the trick finally. They were all well advanced into middle age, save Sissi, who coughed a lot and was incredibly skinny and was affectionately named 'Miss Skimmed Milk' by the others, who mothered her, on account of her non-existent breasts. Of the other three, only Trina stood out on account of her infectious laugh, expensive gold molars and red silk knickers, trimmed with black lace, of which she was inordinately proud and displayed at every available occasion, appropriate or otherwise. 'The real thing,' she would proclaim, when asked. 'Genuine Brussels lace. Brought back from Belgium for me by an old playmate from Berlin. Died in the saddle, he did, but his last words to me were, "It's been worth it, Trina!",' and off she would go in peals of beery laughter.

'The best pieces, kilo for kilo, at the price, yer can get in the whole of Berlin, Count,' Otto had said proudly.

The Count had agreed, beaming now. 'Yes, a fine body of women, Otto. Patriotic, too, leaving their families and homes like this to serve our brave boys abroad, in spite of the dangers.' He had sighed and said sadly, 'I wish I were ten years younger, but alas the spirit is willing, but the flesh.' He had given a little shrug.

Trina had flashed those famous red knickers of hers and given him a gold-toothed seductive smile so that he had brightened up immediately, tugging at the tie of his new 'business suit', saying gruffly, 'Who knows, Otto, while there's life, there's hope. As the old Arab proverb has it, "I cried because I had no boots until I saw a man with no feet".' And with that enigmatic statement, they had commenced their long, slow journey to the frontier with Occupied France.

At the frontier Otto half-expected some sort of trouble. But the ancient, green-clad border-guards had only been curious about the mobile brothel and the girls, muttering as they stalked about it, while Otto and the Count waited nervously for permission to move on, 'If we'd only had something like this in the old war, we'd have shown the buck-teethed Tommies in 1918' and 'Progress, aint it marvellous! *Gash on wheels*, what will they think of next up there in Berlin?'

It was just about then that Trina had flashed those famous red drawers of hers. Some of the old men had flushed and lowered their gazes hastily. Others had applauded politely, while the NCO in charge had hurried inside his hut to present the girls with two bottles of confiscated *Pernod*, bowing slightly and saying, 'Keep up the good work, young ladies!' A few moments later a couple of them had raised the red-and-white striped pole that marked the new German frontier and they were on their way.

Now they rested the sweating, gleaming horses at the top of the long incline which led from German-held Metz, far down below behind them in the valley.

'*La belle France!*' the Count exclaimed expansively, stretching out his arms dramatically, as if he wished to embrace the rolling green Lorraine countryside, dozing in the soft September sunshine. 'The country of my mis-spent youth. Then I came as a visitor, Otto, my boy. Alas now I come as a conqueror.' He sighed.

Otto shook his head firmly. 'No, Count, we don't. We come as humble purveyors of female flesh. Entertainers, if you wish?'

The Count beamed at him. 'Well-put Otto, well-put indeed!'

For a few minutes they sat there on the cab in silence, listening to the sound of the wind over the lonely heights of Gravellotte and the drunken little shrieks and giggles of the girls in the back. Undoubtedly they were well into the second bottle of *Pernod* by this time.

Otto stared out at the faint smudge of the Verdun hills, set against a perfect deep-blue autumn sky and breathed out a sigh of relief. They had done it! At last he was free of that flashy, triumphant Germany with its vulgar brown-shirted, black-booted, brutal confidence. Now he could submerge himself in a new life and a new country, the war forgotten, concerned solely with the business of making money and not the bloody horror of killing on the battlefield. Abruptly he felt almost light-headed with happiness. 'Count,' he cried gaily, flicking his whip against the slick rump of the lead horse to get it moving once more, 'to use an old German phrase – from now onwards, we're going to live like the king in France!'

The Count's eyes sparkled, infected by Otto's sudden enthusiasm, as the mobile brothel started to creak forward once more. 'By God, you're right, Otto,' he agreed. 'Of course, *live like the king in France!*'

Behind them in the rumbling van, the whores

shrieked suddenly with drunken laughter. Why Otto did not know nor care. All that mattered now was that they had pulled it off. They had left the war behind them and the future was bright with hope.